DESCEND

DARK ANGEL ACADEMY SERIES: BOOK ONE

G. BAILEY

JOIN BAILEY'S PACK TO CHAT WITH ME!

Join my Facebook group, <u>Bailey's Pack</u> to stay in touch with me, find out what is coming out next, exclusive teasers, and signed paperback giveaways!

Edits by Polished Perfection

Cover design by Sanja Balan Of Sanja's Covers

❀ Created with Vellum

To the angel that saved me. I believe in you and thank you.

Welcome to The Angel Academy. The only way to be accepted is to die.

My name is Kaitlyn Lightson, and I can see ghosts. Despite my weird ability, which no one but my best friend knows about, my life has been pretty normal. In a few months, I'd be at university and far away from the small ghost town I've lived my whole life in. But one deadly car accident changed everything.

Death was not the end for me, because instead, I became an angel. Guardian Angel to be exact, and my only job is to protect important humans in dire need to pay back the debt of our second life. Only if I can survive Angel Academy, that is.

Turns out Angel Academy is deadlier than any school I've been to before...

I have to choose a side, light or dark, at the end of my first year.

Light angels are good, kind and the choice my best friend is sure to make.
Dark angels are evil, seductive, and they call me to me more than I want to admit.

Seduction is a game in this world, and dark angels know how to play it better than most.
And I want to play.

18+ RH Bully Academy Romance.

He gave me wings when I wanted fire.
"Rise, not burn," he whispered.
-Sara Singhal

CHAPTER 1

"You have popcorn in your hair, did you know that?" the spirit I'm pretending I can't see asks me for the fourth time, his form flickering in and out like a broken lightbulb. He continues to put his hand through my hair, even though we are both aware he can't actually touch me. Between the gaping hole in his chest and the old-fashioned clothes, I suspect he has been here a long time and he has no intention of leaving anytime soon. I knew it was a bad idea to try this place when the cinema in our town was closed. New places *always* mean new ghosts.

But I wanted one date. Just one normal date where the weird fact I can see ghosts and talk to them doesn't bother me, but of course, that didn't happen. Finally, the movie, which I have no clue what happened in, finishes and the end credits roll down the screen. My poor date stares at me hopefully, and I'm pretty sure he is thinking I'm the worst date ever. Jordan O'Moran is a cute guy with messy red hair, blue eyes that pop, and soft looking lips. Not that I would know what they feel like, considering the ghost hasn't left me alone, and touching someone else's skin means trouble when a ghost is around. Sometimes they can see the ghost with me, and sometimes they just pass out. I stand up and tap the shoulder of Riley Becker, my best friend in the entire world and the only one who knows my secret.

Well, the only one that knows my secret and *believes* me. My therapist is proof of how crackers my mum and dad think I am. Currently Riley's tongue is diving down Mandy Maguire's neck, so he hasn't noticed me. For a second, I'm jealous of Riley. He gets to be a normal eighteen-year-old. They both snap out of it at the same time, and Riley stands up, brushing a hand through his wispy blond hair that is all over the place, with questioning eyes.

"Code ten," I whisper to him as we walk through the seats, and Riley looks back at me, nodding once.

"Wanna come back to mine, Riley? My parents work night shifts, so they won't be home," Mandy asks when we get outside. I think the only legit reason Riley asked her out is because she tells the entire school about her empty house and low standards. Riley towers over us both with his lanky six-foot form, and Mandy looks up at him so lovingly. That is until Riley talks.

"I can't. I promised my bestie I'd stay over at hers while her parents are working away. Sorry, another time maybe?" he replies, and Mandy's blue eyes flicker over to me, pure annoyance flashing in them. My mum always says eyes are the windows to the soul, and I'm certain Mandy's soul is thinking of ways to get rid of mine.

"Can I come back to yours?" Jordan asks me, touching my arm. I practically jump away from him, and he looks so confused. Poor guy. For a moment, I actually forgot he was still here. I glance down the empty street outside the cinema, smelling the piles of rubbish by the side of the road, hearing nothing but very distant cars and an owl hunting somewhere in the nearby fields. Thankfully, the chill from the ghost is gone, and he isn't following. *Score.*

About ten years ago, this town would have been full of people; the cinema would have had dozens of people leaving it, but now there is no one but us. Most people live in the big cities these days, and only the rich get to live in the towns, with their kids, of course, like us. Fortunately, my mum and dad are saints with their dozens of charities and thousands of homes they have bought and given to people in need. When I turn twenty-one and finish college, I'm going to help them and hopefully set up my own charity with Riley. That's the game plan anyway.

"Mandy, you live down Tuckers Lane, right? Why don't you take Jordan back with you as he lives close by?" Riley speaks for me when I don't say a word.

Mandy and Jordan look between me and Riley before they both blurt out the same question at the exact same time. "Is there something going on between you two?"

"Nope," I say with a chuckle, and Riley sighs, wrapping his arm around my shoulders.

"Poor Katy couldn't handle me if she tried," he cheekily replies, resting his head on top of mine.

"Plus, he is a brother to me; we literally grew up in each other's houses," I remind Mandy and Jordan. Riley and I... It just isn't like that.

"Right..." Jordan mutters and walks off with Mandy following behind him, tugging her short skirt down so her ass doesn't pop out. Jordan grins at Mandy, and she steps a little closer as she laughs at something he said.

"Our dates are totally going to bang tonight, aren't they?" I ask Riley, who grins down at me.

"Totally," he replies and laughs. His laugh makes me feel better about ruining his night. The date was over for me the second the ghost sensed me, like they all do, and decided to try and get me to talk to him all night.

"We suck at dates," I mumble, feeling guilty as I tuck a strand of my wavy blonde hair behind my ear.

"Well, I could have been sucked, but our ghost friend ruined that. What happened?" he replies, and I screw my face up.

"One, gross," I mutter. "And two, the ghost just hovered in front of me throughout the whole movie, trying to pick popcorn out of my hair but failing. I couldn't see the movie," I explain. Riley leans down and picks some of the popcorn caught up in my curly blonde locks that bounce around everywhere. Dad likes to joke that he fell in love with my mum because of her curly blonde hair and how he could store his snacks in there and she wouldn't know. I push my waist-length hair behind my back and out of Riley's hand, sighing.

"That's shit, Katy, has the ghost not moved on?" he asks me, looking around, not that he can see them. Sometimes the ghosts are strong enough that

Riley can feel the coldness, the feel of death as I call it.

"There's a light near him, but he doesn't look at it like the ones who are going to move on," I explain, as that's really the only way to describe the light. Some ghosts have a light nearby, and many of them spend days staring at the light before going into it and disappearing. Others have a swirling black circle near them, and they are forever running from it. I gather the light is what some people call heaven, and the dark must be hell.

Or some version of it.

I think true hell is in the minds of the lost souls with nowhere to go...forever trapped, watching the world go by.

"You want to drive?" Riley asks, holding his keys in the air, the shiny Iron Man helmet keyring hanging inches away from my fingers. I won him that keyring when we were twelve and his dad took me, Riley and Riley's younger sister to Blackpool.

That was the only good part of the trip...turns out Blackpool has a lot of ghosts.

"Really?" I snap the keys out of his hand and run through the car park, pressing the button to unlock the car doors. Riley's red Land Rover sits in the corner of the lot, and I climb into the driver's seat, messing with the seat height as Riley gets in. I love Riley's car; it's so much better than the tiny pink Mini Cooper that my parents got me.

I hate pink for starters, but I couldn't tell my parents that. They went to so much effort to find me the car in the first place.

"See, I knew this would put a smile on your face," Riley comments, knocking my shoulder with his, and I grin at him. Riley just gets me. I start the car up and change the gears as we leave the car park and head down the empty country road to home. The Lake District is beautiful, but it's miles between anything out here. I leave my full beam lights on as Riley turns the radio station on, making me shift my eyes to his birthmark on his wrist, the one that looks like angel wings. I have one nearly exactly like it on the inside of my thigh, but mine is a lot bigger, taking up nearly all my thigh. Riley jokes that we were destined to be best friends, and who knows, maybe he was right.

"Are you going to ask Jordan out again?" Riley asks, relaxing back in his seat.

"Nope. We both are on summer break, but it's nearly September," I remind him. Riley has certainly had his summer fun, while I've been in my house, mainly reading. I think back to the book I left half read earlier today, a paranormal romance about—

"What book are you thinking about?"

"How do you know I was thinking about a book?"

"Because I know you, Katy—" Anything Riley was going to say is lost as the car harshly slams into something, and the world seems to slow down. With wide eyes, I grip the steering wheel tightly in my hand and scream as the car seems to float for a moment. In the silence, in the moment where I'm sure I'm floating, I reach for my best friend.

And then everything goes black.

CHAPTER 2

"She doesn't scream like the others. How...fascinating." A deep, albeit hazy, voice drifts to my ears as I lie in something hot, something burning me right down to my soul. I immediately open my eyes and try to sit up, but I can't see anything except white light and I can't move. A scream escapes my lips, even though I try to keep it in, as the pain extends from my back, all across my body until there is nothing but the feeling of fire in the pitch-black room. Within seconds the pain is gone, and I fall through the air, slamming solidly onto cold stone as light blasts into my eyes, making them hurt. I curl up, pulling my knees to my naked chest as I dart my eyes around the stone room I'm in. Strange white symbols that look like they are on fire are drawn into the stone around the room, and there must be thousands of them. Looking up, I see white fire in a ball above me, burning so brightly like a star. It's beautiful, and I find myself staring at it like it can give me some answers to the hundreds of questions running around in my mind.

Was I inside that?

Where are my clothes?

Where the frigging hell am I?

The sound of wood dragging across stone makes me snap my gaze behind me as the only door to the room opens and a man in a white cloak steps in. He has waist-length, straight black hair that somehow doesn't look feminine at all on him. His hazel eyes watch me under his thick black eyelashes, and I would guess he is in his thirties.

Wait, not a man.

An angel.

White fluffy wings hang off his shoulders, big enough to drop onto the floor behind him. He walks towards me and, to my surprise, sits down on the stone and offers me a white cloak with a pair of white shorts. I eye the clothes in his hands for only a moment before I take them, feeling the silky material under my hands. I carefully put the clothes on, pulling my hair out of the top of the cloak and tucking it around me as I sit still.

"Yes, angels exist, and in the world you grew up in, there was much magic around you," the angel says first. No explanation to why I'm here, just a statement about there being more magical beings in the world other than me. I wonder if angels can see ghosts.

Lifting my gaze from the ground, I search his calm hazel eyes. "I can see angels exist, clearly...unless you are very good at making costumes. Why did you tell me that?"

"Usually that's the first question everyone asks. Was it not going to be yours?" he enquires, tilting his head to the side, some amusement and interest in his expression.

When you see ghosts all the time, believing angels are real is nothing. But old habits die hard, so I don't tell him that.

"I was going to ask who the hell you are and why you kidnapped me," I state, crossing my arms. "If you are part of some cloak wearing cult group, you have the wrong person. I legit will be the worst member ever."

To my surprise, he laughs, a soft laugh that makes me want to relax. I don't though, I'm not stupid. "Young people, you do amuse me so." He is still laughing, and I glare at him long enough that he clears his throat, a big smile still on his lips. "We did not kidnap you, and we are not a cult, Kaitlyn Lightson."

"That's exactly what a cult would say," I point out, and it only seems to amuse him more. I arch an eyebrow, and he sighs, his smile dropping.

"What is the last thing you remember, Miss Lightson?" he asks, and until then, I don't know why I didn't remember.

The car...it crashed, and then there was nothing but darkness until the pain of the fire. I was in the damn fire?

Did they drag me out of the car and bring me here? And why would the angels do that? I suppose I've always been worried my powers would put me in danger one day, but I assumed it would be because of a psycho ghost and not an angel kidnapping cult.

"Riley and I were in a car. I was driving, and I'm sure we crashed into something," I mumble, running the last few moments of the crash over and over. There was something in the road, but I wasn't looking. It was my fault. I snap my eyes to the angel. "Wait, where is Riley? Why aren't I in a hospital? Where are my parents?"

"Please do calm down, Miss Lightson. Mr. Riley

Becker is fine, and your parents are on earth, where they should be," he starts to explain, and I feel like the ball is about to drop right before it actually does. "Miss Lightson, your human soul and body died in the car crash on the sixteenth of August 2019. It was a tragic and predestined accident that happened to twenty people at the exact same time all over the earth, and I am sorry for your loss. Now—"

I stop him because this shit sounds unbelievable. "How could I have died if I'm right here, you know, *alive*?"

"I was getting to that. Please don't interrupt until the end," he suggests, and I frown but keep quiet. "The angel birthmark on your thigh is called an angel blessing. Any baby born with an angel blessing will die between the ages of eighteen and twenty-one in a predestined tragedy. The young adult is then reborn in holy fire, and they become an angel in training, an opportunity to become something incredible. A blessing in death, you might say." He points a finger into the air, and I look up, lost in the beauty of the white fire for a moment again.

"Are you suggesting I was reborn in that white fire and I'm now an angel?" I ask, and then I laugh. I'm still laughing as I stand up, shaking my head. "Right, you are crazy, and I need to go home now."

He shakes his head, a serious edge appearing in his eyes. "My name is Professor Badhur, and I am one of the many teachers here at The Angel Academy. You will learn more in the welcoming ceremony ahead of you, but there is something important I must explain to you before that."

"Which is?"

"The holy fire saved your soul, and now you owe a debt to the light above. If you try to run away, kill another angel or break any of the rules given to you, you will be killed. This is your second chance at life, Miss Lightson, do not fail at it," he gravely tells me. "If you pass The Angel Academy, you will be paired with another angel and given a human to watch over until their deaths. As you are now immortal, many humans will be your charges."

I'm speechless as I stare at him for a long time, hearing the distant sound of chatter and water dripping. "You're not lying, are you?"

"Light angels do not lie; it taints our souls, and it is the deal we made for our wings," he tells me as he walks to the door and holds it open for me. "The next part of your angel life is yours. If you do not wish to live it, then stay in this room, and I will end your life. If you wish to fight for this chance, walk out of this door with your head held high and find your destiny."

I stare at the door for a second, but I already know my choice.

I might not understand everything, but the only way I'm getting answers is by finding them, even if it means accepting whatever I now am. I walk to the door, and Professor Badhur bows his head at me. "Blessed be the angels."

"Blessed be the angels," I find myself replying before I step out of the room and into my new life.

CHAPTER 3

The cold from the stone under my feet makes me hyperaware of everything as I walk down the dimly lit corridor towards the warm yellow light at the other end. I can hear whispered voices somewhere nearby, I can smell blood and sweat, like it sticks to the walls, and I feel a tiny amount of damp that itches my nose. I shiver as I get closer to the end of the corridor, where there is a frosted glass door, making it impossible to see anything but warm yellow light on the other side. The door has a silver handle, and the light coming from behind it flickers every now and then like a fire would. I look back down the corridor, seeing that I'm completely alone and the professor never followed me out.

God, I'm scared.

I calm my shaky hands as I turn the handle of the door and pull it open, feeling a blast of heat across all of my skin, followed by the hushed whispers. Two hooded angels stand right in front of the door, both wearing white cloaks with long hoods that hide their faces. The only difference is their wings. One of them has white wings, much like Professor Badhur, and the other has pitch black wings that remind me of a starless night sky. At the same time, they step aside and stretch their hands out in front of them, and only then do I realise the massive room I've just walked into. It's a dome made out of stained glass with a stone floor and seating all around the edges, making the room look like an arena.

The seats are filled to the brim with angels, and there is a clear divide between each of the sections. Angels with white wings all sit in one part, and then there is a row of empty seats before the section of people that look like normal people with no wings. Then another gap before angels with black wings sit all together. There must be a thousand people in the room, and all their eyes are on me as I walk down past the seats and into the clearing in the centre. There are twenty people sat on chairs, and right at the back, there is one empty seat. Every single one of the twenty people look as young as I do as they all stare, and I look between each one of them before I see the one familiar pair of eyes I didn't know I was looking for.

"Riley." I whisper his name like a prayer, relief filling my steps as I go to the remaining chair next to him and sit down. Riley wordlessly stares at me, and then he smiles in relief, and I let out the breath I was holding in. I smile back, not knowing what else to do as the two angels who walked me in move to stand in front of the group, and they slowly take down their hoods. Riley's little finger hooks in mine, comforting me when we both know we need to be quiet.

Whatever is going on, we will fix it together. It's what best friends do.

"My name is Professor Louton, and welcome to The Angel Academy," the angel with black wings comments. She is young with bright blonde hair, a long nose and a very serious expression. Her purple eyes look like they might have been bright once, but now darkness tints them, matching the rest of her. The other angel looks a lot older with long grey hair and expressionless features. He simply just stands there, looking at something above our heads and ignoring the world. "I am a dark angel, and Master Gabriel at my side is a light angel. Your first year at

Angel Academy is designed to test your nature and for you to find an answer to the most important question in your life now."

"The choice between light and dark. You must choose which wings and which side of your new soul you wish to fully take," Master Gabriel follows up, his words echoing around the room.

"More will become apparent as the year carries on, and at the end, you will choose a side. You will each try to spend three years at The Angel Academy, learning what you need to become a Guardian Angel to an important human being," Professor Louton continues and clears her throat.

"What happens if you don't want to do this? What happens if you fail at something?" I ask into the brief silence, and it goes so quiet in the room that I wonder if I should have kept my mouth shut.

"You die, lass," Master Gabriel answers me, none too kindly at all.

"If you successfully finish The Angel Academy, you will have a brilliant life and find your place in the world of the angels. Welcome to Neamh, the home of the angels, and blessed be the angels," Professor Louton says, and every angel in the room repeats her parting words as I look towards Riley.

"What the frigging hell do we do next?" I whisper. "This is some messed up cult shit. We need to escape."

"No clue, Katy, but it isn't a cult. Okay, maybe it is, but doesn't being an angel sound pretty cool?" he asks, and I look away. No, it doesn't because I didn't choose this.

And I don't like the sound of the price we are going to pay to the light above. Whatever the heck that is.

"All new students, please make a line and follow after me, and the students finishing their year one must stay behind to make their choice. Master Gabriel will be guiding you, and blessed be the angels no matter which side you pick," Professor Louton states, and nearly every student gets up right away, including Riley. I only get up when he pulls on my arm, and we get into the line that follows Professor Louton back into the corridor we came from. There is laughter from the other angels in the room, and I follow the sound to clash my gaze with a pair of golden flame-filled eyes, just before I head into the corridor and out of sight.

Tugging Riley's arm towards me, I whisper, "Where do you think they are taking us?"

"Nowhere good, that I'm sure of. I'm Vesnia Burns," a girl right behind me answers for Riley, and

I look back, seeing her curly red hair that reminds me of my own hair, except that it is as red as blood. Her eyes are nearly black but with tints of brown, and her pale-skinned face is covered in freckles.

"I actually agree with you. I'm Kaitlyn Lightson, and this is my best friend, Riley Becker," I reply.

"You're lucky you came in here with someone," she answers, her eyes nervously looking around.

"I don't think any of us are lucky," I whisper back as cold air blows around my cloak, and we get to the end of the corridor, where nothing but a cliff edge and the brisk night sky greet us.

"Stand in a line by the edge. Be careful," Professor Louton demands, and reluctantly I do as she asks, standing between Riley and Vesnia. The cold is brutal as my bare feet dig into the flat stone below me.

"Do you see creatures flying below you?" Professor Louton asks. I lean over the edge just a little bit as everyone else does, and I'm shocked silent by the sight in front of us. In the night sky, hundreds of horses of many different colours fly around the clouds, disappearing in and out of them. I can't see the ground, and it makes me wonder exactly how high up we are. "These are flying horses, and they are gifts for new angels. They will be your familiars, yours to look after and trust in. Now catch one."

"What do you mean—" Vesnia asks just as something hard slams into my back, and I scream as I fall off the edge of the cliff.

CHAPTER 4

The arctic air bites and scrapes against my skin, filling my lungs like I just swallowed a jug of ice water, and every part of my body freezes in pure shock. My tears disappear in the wind as I rapidly fall, spinning around in circles until I stretch my arms and legs out, hoping to stop it. I force my eyes open, looking down to see the horses below me and how they are flying around, and some are super close. Underneath them are tall mountains, again all filled with flying horses that fly around them. A nearby scream reaches my ears, and I look to my left to see Riley and five other students rapidly falling. I try to move my body towards him, but a gush of wind sends me spiralling to the right and losing sight of Riley altogether. I gasp as I fall right past a horse who moves to dodge me, and I try to breathe and think.

They wouldn't just want to kill us.

This has to be a test...and what could they want? I look back up at the horse I just passed, Professor Louton's words drifting back to me.

"THESE ARE FLYING HORSES, *and they are gifts for new angels. They will be your familiars, yours to look after and trust in. Now catch one.*"

CATCH ONE? *How the frigging heck am I meant to do that?* I look down, seeing two brown horses right under me, and I mentally try to steel myself for landing on one of them. Inches before I reach my hands out for the horse's mane, the horse flies away, leaving me tumbling down in the air. I scream, spinning around and taking a few precious seconds to flatten myself again against the air and look for another horse. I glance at the mountains below me and see a horse right on the tip of the highest mountain, its white fur shining, reflecting the moonlight.

Perfect.

It's already still and landed, which should make this easier if I can just get near enough. Flattening my hands on my body, just like I've seen in action movies, I direct my body towards the tip of the high mountain and right towards the horse. As I get closer, it turns its gaze and looks up at me. The horse's white wings spread out as we lock gazes, and I beg whoever is listening that this horse doesn't move. My heart feels like it is in my stomach as I get so close, knowing this is going to hurt as I land. I'm inches away from the horse when the horse moves it wings and takes off. Tears sting my eyes as I see the snow below me, knowing there is no way I'm going to survive this.

I'm sorry, mum and dad.

I'm sorry, Riley, you're on your own.

I'm—

My thoughts are cut off as suddenly the horse is below me, and I land on its back with a thud, smacking my head against its back hard enough to make me dizzy. I lock my hands onto the horse's mane as I sit up, the world looking fuzzy as we literally fly on top of it.

"Hello, you saved me," I whisper to my horse in pure relief. A smile fills my lips as I glance around, seeing Riley on a brown horse, flying right towards me. In the distance, I see Vesnia on a black horse with a long grey mane, and she waves at me.

A long whistle sounds in the distance, and my horse takes off, flying in the same direction as all the others with riders. I look back once, my smile dropping from my lips as I see two students' bodies on the mountain, snowflakes falling on their lifeless bodies as blood spreads around them in the white snow.

What kind of academy is this?

THE HORSES FLY UP for a long time through the clouds, and I keep my eyes high until we break out of the clouds and into the night sky, and there's a castle floating in the middle of it. The castle sits on a floating rock, and around the castle looks like a jungle full of thick trees of all different colours. There are a few small houses around it and beautiful gardens in between them. The castle itself is stunning, like *straight out of a Disney movie* stunning. The castle has what must be dozens of white spired towers and bridges connecting all of the castle to the main part in the middle. When I look up expecting to see the moon, instead, it's a floating orb of intense light, with angels in a line like a barrier all the way around it. The orb is shining the same light that the moon would give off, but I doubt we are on earth anymore. It certainly doesn't feel like it. I stare longer at the orb, and I soon realise the angels around it aren't real, they are made of stone.

I get a strange urge to fly up and touch them, but another loud whistle gets our horses' attention. My eyes just briefly meet Riley's before the horses are swooping down, taking all the air from my lungs at the same time. I hold on as tightly as I can, fearing I'm going to fall off any second, and when I open my eyes, I see we are flying around the castle and getting lower each time. The other horses form a line behind me, and my horse is the first to land right in front of an angel with a whistle in her mouth, which she drops and smiles at me.

"Welcome, new students! I am Professor Nina, and I will be teaching you everything there is to know about your new horse familiar. For now, please come and collect a whistle necklace and secure your bond as I'm sure none of you want to be pushed off a cliff again!" She laughs as she speaks, like it's funny.

It's frigging not.

My horse seems to understand and walks

forward before lowering down so I can slide off easily, the horse's wings brushing against my cheek.

"Congratulations, Miss Lightson. This horse is almost legendary among us angels. No one has ever been able to catch her, and she has been around almost as long as Master Gabriel," Professor Nina comments, smiling at me, but something darker twinkles in her eyes. My aunt used to tell me just because something looks like sugar doesn't mean it's not salt. "Now press your hand onto your horse's head and learn her name." I nod and lift my hand, placing it on the side of the horse's head. Suddenly an ear-splitting voice speaks into my mind, and a warm feeling travels around my chest.

Ayda.

"Her name is Ayda," I whisper, lowering my hand and seeing an angel blessing mark on her fur, and it glows a white colour.

"A lovely name. Now here is your whistle, and you may ask Ayda to go and rest while I work with the other students," she tells me and walks away.

"Thank you for catching me, Ayda. I guess I owe you a favour, because what kind of angel can't catch herself?"

Ayda neighs at me before running off, stretching her long white wings into the air and taking off into the sky. I slip the silver chain around my neck, letting the thin, silver, star-shaped whistle hang on my chest as I look up at the castle, which is meant to be my new home.

Welcome to The Angel Academy.

CHAPTER 5

Twiddling with the whistle necklace, I stare up at the tall towers of The Angel Academy as we follow Professor Nina inside. The doors are made of pure clouded glass, and the warmth of the inside makes my cheeks burn as I stare around. The room is a giant square with at least six dark wood staircases disappearing up and down to other floors. The walls are littered with paintings, hundreds of them, and in every single painting there is an angel.

Self-absorbed much?

The floor below our feet is shiny, glossy wood that creaks with every step we take through this large space. We all stop right in the middle of the room, and Riley stays close to my side.

"One second, we are just waiting on someone,"

Professor Nina explains from the staircase she stands in the middle of.

"On a scale of one to ten, how much did you freak out when we were pushed off that cliff?" Riley whispers to me.

"About one hundred on the scale of *let's never talk about the cliff again*," I tightly reply, knowing he is joking, but I don't have it in me to see any of this as humorous. "Aren't you upset? Our parents think we are dead, and we can't tell them we are okay."

"We have been given a second chance at life, Katy. Nothing else matters," he replies with a big smile before looking back to Professor Nina. I run my gaze over the students with us and, to my annoyance, nearly all of them look happy. *Not a brainwashing cult, my ass.*

Except for one redhead girl with a frown on her face. Vesnia's eyes meet mine through the four people between us, and I see the same sorrow in her eyes. The same words I want to scream from the top of my lungs. The same fight in us. I know neither of us are going to give up without a fight, and we aren't going to accept that we can't see our families again. We have to get back to our families and tell them the truth of what happened. My mum and dad deserve that much, even if Riley can't see that right now.

"Sorry I'm late, Professor Nina. We will take it from here," a girl exclaims, sounding like an overenthusiastic cheerleader before I even look at her. I go to look at the girl who is still talking, but the boy next to her draws all my attention.

Not boy...man...dark angel. Drool-worthy dark angel. The guy stands straight, his arms crossed against his leather jacket with a crown pin on the collar, hiding the no doubt trained body underneath. Black wings rest right behind him, gracefully touching the floor by his feet. I slowly look past his thick arms to his chiselled jawline that looks like an artist sculpted him, then above his soft pale lips to his thick black hair that has a slight curl to the end of his locks. Only, when I search his eyes, I find them staring right back at me.

Eyes that look like sparks of embers once burned there on the face of an angel. Total girl trap.

But nope, not this girl. This girl has bigger things to focus on than an angel.

Maybe.

His lips tilt up, looking almost amused as my eyes bounce between him and the girl still talking as I keep dragging my eyes away from him and forcing myself to look away to the girl. All blonde hair, big boobs that don't look real, and skinny legs in a tiny mini skirt, she is exactly what I expected her to look like. Oddly, there is a crown pin on her soft white jumper, just like the guy's.

"I'm Jessica Weven, and this is Henry Ravaric, and we are the king and queen of the academy," she exclaims, and I roll my eyes. Figures hot guy one and happy-happy cheerleader are some kind of leaders. Why couldn't a geeky angel lead for a change?

"Not literally, right?" I ask before I can stop myself, and then everyone stares at me like I just shouted that I'm naked or something.

"Literal in every sense, darlin'," Henry replies, his voice as deep, gravelly and sexy as I thought it might be. The London accent is familiar, and everything about him puts me on edge as much as it makes me want to move closer.

"Yes, the titles of queen and king are given to the angels who beat the previous queen or king in a battle of sorts," Jessica claims, and she looks damn proud of herself.

"Like a head boy and girl then?" Vesnia asks.

"Exactly, but with more power," Jessica replies, sounding pleased, but my eyes are fixed on Henry as he still stares. "Now girls come with me, boys with Henry. We are going to show you to your rooms, and then in the morning, there will be someone to take you on a tour."

Henry looks to the left where another older angel is waiting, and he steps forward. "Everyone leave except for the mouthy one. Boys go with Duke here."

I scoff, crossing my arms. "You mean me, angel?"

"Katy didn't mean to be mouthy, did you?" Riley tensely asks, wrapping an arm over my shoulder, and Henry watches Riley's arm like it's a snake.

"I meant every word. A self-appointed king is nothing other than a man with a crown," I point out.

"Careful, Miss Kaitlyn Lightson. Your king is always watching." With that threat, he walks through the crowd of students who part like the sea for their king.

And for some reason, my sarcastic lips move before I can even stop them.

"Watch away, your highness." Thankfully, he doesn't reply to me and disappears down some stairs, with the boys of our class following, except for Riley.

"Can you not get yourself killed for the rest of the night, please?" he asks, moving right in front of me and a tad bit too close. His hands rest on my shoulders as I meet his eyes.

"I'm going to be sleeping; how could I get into any trouble?" I ask, and he rolls his eyes.

"Go and behave." He pushes me in the direction of the staircase the girls went down. I hurry to the stairs and walk down, where Vesnia and Jessica are waiting for me. Jessica looks at me with interest and tilts her head to the corridor.

"This is the girls' section, and the only way in or out is this staircase. It is also magically cursed so that boys can't walk down them without being in intense pain," she explains with a long sigh. "It totally sucks, and the staircase to the boys' section is cursed as well so that girls can't walk down it either."

"It's actually pretty smart," Vesnia points out, and Jessica rolls her eyes.

"*Anyway*, every two rooms share a bathroom, and these two are the last rooms left on this level. There are more rooms down the back, but they haven't been used in ages," she explains, lifting her hand and checking out her nails as she talks.

"Right, where do you sleep then?" I ask, counting only twenty doors.

"The four end doors lead to corridors with better rooms. You get upgraded when you choose your wings and you need a balcony. You don't need one until then, obviously, newbie," she explains with a sarcastic laugh.

"Not unless they plan to push us off a cliff again," Vesnia groans, walking to the door marked Room Seventeen. "See you in the bathroom, Katy. Bye, Jessica."

"See ya," I reply with a smile just for her. I walk to the door that is number nineteen, and it's ironic this is my room number when I'm never going to be nineteen. I died before I got a chance.

"Wait," Jessica whispers, stepping closer to me. With a smile like a cat about to eat a mouse, she leans close, careful not to touch me, her black wings stretching out ever so softly. Now that I finally see why she has dark wings, the darkness in her eyes is easy to see. "The king always belongs to the queen, got it?"

"You might want to tell the king that," I chuckle as I turn the handle to my room and head inside.

CHAPTER 6

The smell of dust, cleaning products and cotton flitter through my senses as I step into my dark room and feel the wall by the door for a light switch. After a few seconds in the dark, I find the switch and flick it on. Bright light floods my eyes, making me blink a few times before I can focus on the room which is now my new home. It's a studio apartment with a white wooden framed double bed taking up most the room, along with the blue fabric sofa pushed up against the end of it. The bed has white sheets in a pile on the end with two pillows next to it. There is a large window on the other side of the room with another door on the right wall, which I'm guessing goes to the shared bathroom. A wardrobe on the other side takes up another big chunk of the room.

I look to my right, and I'm surprised to see two suitcases that look like my own suitcases from home, next to an empty white desk. I feel frozen as I stare at them before I shake myself out of it and rush to my suitcases. I push them onto the floor and open the red one first, finding all my clothes inside. I almost bury my head into them, just because it's great to have a touch of home here. I unlock the second suitcase and find the handstitched blanket that my mum made for me for my twelfth birthday. I clutch the woven blue and black material and lift it up and wrap it around my shoulders like mum always used to do. I chuckle when I see a box of Parma Violets sweets in the suitcase next to a pile of my romance books and my Kindle. I get a packet of the sweets that I adore to the point of obsession as someone knocks once.

"Bathroom roomie, can I come in?" Vesnia's voice comes through the other door.

"Sure!" I shout back and make my way to sit down on the sofa, curling my feet under me as Vesnia comes in, wearing pyjama shorts with pizzas on them and a top that says, "Pizza is life" on it.

"Okay, I thought all this was weird, for the record, but the suitcases full of our things?" Vesnia shakes her head. "My dad never would have let anyone in my room to take my stuff. Especially not if he thought..."

"Same here. My mum and dad wouldn't have given this stuff up," I mutter, rubbing my head. I open the sweets and chew on one, offering Vesnia a sweet, but she screws her nose up.

"Ew, no. I hate those sweets," she says in disgust.

"Good, it means we can be friends. I don't like sharing anything," I reply before I eat another sweet, and we both laugh for a moment.

"Call me Ves. My friends used to..." she drifts off before clearing her throat. "Well, my old friends, I guess."

"Okay, Ves," I answer with a sad smile. I get it.

"I'm going to get some sleep. I'm exhausted, but I wanted to check on you," Ves says, heading for the door. "We are in this together, right? We should keep an eye on each other as I have a feeling this place is pretty on the outside but dark everywhere else."

"Right. I have your back, Ves," I tell her honestly, and I slightly agree with her.

"I have yours too," she replies with a big grin before leaving my room. I pop another sweet into my mouth, deciding I need to make my bed and then get some sleep, just as a deep voice makes all the hairs on the back of my neck stand up.

"The new ones are going to die." I swiftly turn around, seeing a ghost in front of the window. The ghost's back is to me, leaving me only to see his black, very expensive looking suit and dark hair. He isn't as see-through as the usual ghosts I see, and he has a strange white glow to him, much unlike the usual red, blue or green colours I see on the ghosts. I search around him for a light or dark portal, but there isn't anything nearby. Just this ghost watching the star-filled skies. Like the world slows, the ghost turns around and locks eyes with me. Every danger alert I've ever taught myself just disappears as I meet his gaze and stay so still. His hair is the colour of dark smoke, snaking around his forehead in thick locks. His eyes remind me of a twilight sky, touched with purple and blue streaks of light. He is incredibly handsome and strange, a dangerous mixture. I eye his ears and how the tips are pointed up, kind of like an elf.

Is that what he is? An elf?

"You can see me." He leaves the statement, not a question, between us. I never talk to ghosts or meet their gaze like I am right now. Not since I did it as a kid and learnt what happens when ghosts start to haunt you. When I was seven, I made friends with the ghost of a teenager who called herself True. True died in a car crash, and she wanted to find her parents, but I was too young to help her with that. I told her she could be my friend, and for a while, it worked...then she got restless. True started screaming at me all the time, and then it escalated to her pushing me down the stairs and breaking my arm. I ended up having a four-hour surgery to put plates in my arm to fix what True did, and then when I went home, she was gone. Riley said she might have followed me to the hospital and got lost there, but I like to think she moved on to wherever the ghosts go. I rub the three scars on my arm that serve as a reminder of what ghosts can do when they get obsessed.

"Are you an elf?" I ask, and he laughs, like a full-body laugh that is addictive, and I find myself chuckling along with him.

I'm laughing with a ghost. FML.

"Elf? No, not at all. I am a vampire," he replies, and I go very still. I search his body for any sign of injury or what killed him, but I don't find anything. "But that must be our secret for now, or at least until we trust each other more. Angels like yourself do not like the word vampire."

"Why?" I find myself asking. Stop talking to the ghost, Kaitlyn.

"Such a long story, and we have only just met," he replies with a secretive smirk. I bet when he was alive, he could get all the girls with only a smile. Maybe he has a ghost harem...it wouldn't even surprise me. "I'm Erendriel Raloxisys, a master vampire and currently suffering with a dead problem."

I can't help but smile a little at him. Dammit, charming ghosts are a new kind of danger, it seems. "I'm Kaitlyn Lightson, I can see ghosts and have been able to since I was five. I also died, and now I'm apparently training to be an angel."

"Death seems to be our thing in common," he smiles, flashing me a toothy grin in which I see two fangs. Damn, he isn't lying. I'm talking to a vampire ghost, and vampires are real.

What fairy tale isn't real at this point?

"Kaitlyn," he whispers my name, almost like he is tasting it on his lips. I shiver even though the room isn't cold.

"Eren...dr...wait, I'm just going to call you Ren as your name is too complicated," I mutter.

"Ren I like," he replies. "But then, I've not spoken to anyone in what seems like forever, so I am bound to agree with you."

"How long ago did you die?" I ask, taking a step

closer even when the logical side of me tells me I should be running out of this room at full speed.

"Eighty years ago, I came to this castle. I was eighteen, new to my vampire powers, and I thought I could trust the angels. My death in their hands started a war they have won," he growls in anger.

I tilt my head to the side, wondering why I'm so interested in this ghost. I've seen good-looking ghosts before, but I've never been stupid enough to interact with them. "The angels killed you. Why would they do that?"

"If you want me to tell you a secret, you must tell me one back," he counters.

"I don't play games with ghosts, Ren," I sourly reply. He walks closer to me, and I smell a strange scent of cinnamon mixed with a musk rosewood, and it takes me a moment to realise I can smell Ren.

And that's never, *ever* happened before.

Ghosts aren't really here...they don't have scents...they aren't real in this world. I hide my emotions as best I can because he doesn't need to know how I'm freaking the hell out inside.

Becoming an angel? No problem. Smelling a ghost? Yep, total freak out.

"I'm going to play all sorts of games with my new

friend, Kaitlyn Lightson. When you need me, just call."

Then he is just gone, and my room feels emptier than ever, and I finally let my shaky legs sink me onto the floor. One thing is for sure, my heart is not safe in this academy. Neither are my secrets.

CHAPTER 7

"Kat, did you get a breakfast tray too?" Ves shouts through the bathroom door as I finish brushing my hair. I like that we have nicknames for each other when we literally only just met. I guess dying and becoming an angel has a way of bonding people. "Only I hate eating on my own and, well, can I eat with you?" I glance at my skinny jeans, purple tee with "I bite" written on it, and my favourite black Doc Martens that have purple laces in the full mirror by the bathroom door.

"Morning! Come in!" I shout back, and she opens the door as I sit on the edge of my extremely comfy bed. Ves comes and sits by me as I tug my own tray onto my lap and take off the blue lid, revealing two slices of toast, a little cornflake box in a bowl, a bottle of water and a carton of milk.

"Did you sleep well?" Ves asks after she eats her toast. I finish mine off and open the bottle of water, taking a deep gulp before answering her.

"Like an angel," I wink at her, and she laughs, bumping my shoulder. Which is a giant lie. After Ren disappeared, I spent all night thinking about him, worrying about him coming back, and wondering how many ghosts might be lurking around the academy, waiting to scare me. What if they have troll ghosts here? Or freaking dragons? I don't even know if those creatures are real, but I don't want to see their ghosts any time soon.

"It's seriously messed up to think we are actually dead," Ves mumbles.

"How did you die?" I ask, curious about her life. "I mean, if you don't mind telling me. You don't have to, though."

"It's okay," she replies, clearing her throat. "I lived in France, though my family is from Wales, and we moved to France for my dad's job when I was twelve. Hence the weird accent."

"Your accent is nice, though I was curious where it was from," I reply. "Oh wait, can you speak French? That would be cool."

"Nope, I'm terrible at French. I was home-schooled and always the outcast," she admits, biting on her lip. "Anyways, I was bike riding with my dad, something we always did, and it got late. We were heading back when I rode too close to the edge of a cliff. The cliff gave way, and the last thing I remember is my dad screaming my name."

"I'm so sorry, Ves," I say, placing my hand on her arm. "I crashed a car with Riley inside it. We died together, and I don't remember much either."

"I'm sorry too. Where are you from?" she asks, clearly wanting to change the subject a little.

"Lake District. My mum is an artist and met my dad when he bought my mum's painting of a house on the lake. That house was my dad's holiday home, and the rest is history," I explain, and she smiles at me. We both jump as someone bangs our door before shouting through it.

"Time to get up, newbie. Outside in five!"

"Let's hurry and eat," I say, and Ves agrees as she digs into her food. Four minutes later, we walk out of my room and head up the stairs where six other students are waiting. Each of them looks a little less dazed than yesterday and in their own clothes.

"Katy!" Riley shouts my name, and I turn to see him head up the stairs in his usual jeans and a white T-shirt. "You look great." He tugs me into his arms, hugging me a little too tightly and not exactly what

I'm used to. We hug sometimes, but then again, we have been going through a lot these last twenty-four hours. Riley finally lets me go, though he keeps his arm around my higher waist.

"Riley, remember Vesnia?" I ask, and he nods at me, not looking at her once. Before I can call Riley out on his rude behaviour, someone claps their hands. We all turn to see Professor Badhur standing on the steps, the white cloak long gone, and this time, he has a blue shirt on and black trousers, looking pretty normal except for the wings and long hair.

"Welcome, new students, to The Angel Academy. Today there will be no lessons because you are to have a tour around the academy and get to know your new home," he exclaims with a big smile. "Now, there is a map and class schedule for your first year waiting in your room when you return. Until then, I am handing you over to Thallon Cross, who is in charge of the tour. Blessed be the angels, and I will see each of you in my class this week."

"Hello, new students, my name is Thallon Cross, and welcome to The Angel Academy," a man speaks behind us, and we all turn around at the same time to see who spoke. The guy standing a few steps up on the stairs is not what I expected to see. Thallon

Cross has no wings, which is odd, considering where we are, and his eyes are literally glowing a bright white with tints of blue shining through. He snakes a tanned hand through his thick brown hair that is sun-kissed at the tips, and my eyes trace over his full bow-shaped lips and sexy jawline. He has a slight scar under his chin which makes him seem all the more real. I would guess his age around the twenties, but the way he holds himself tall makes me think he is a little older.

What is he?

"He can cross into my panties any day," Vesnia whispers to me, and I chuckle.

"I am an angel before any of you ask. No, I won't tell you why I don't have wings," he answers likely everyone's questions all in one go. "Now follow me and keep up, you don't want to get lost. When the tour is over, I have a surprise for you all in the kitchens in the form of sweets and hot chocolate." The group follows quickly after Thallon as we leave the room and head into a long corridor. Thallon explains which lessons are in here, and then we get to the end of the corridor which leads to a big greenhouse.

"This is one of my favourite rooms of the academy. The greenhouse is dead centre of the building, and there are doors to every part of the academy from here. So basically, if you get lost, find the greenhouse and start over," Thallon explains as we walk past tall plants with big green leaves, and tiny little red flowers in pots that line the paths. Butterflies of all different colours fly over our heads, and birds chirp in the distance. The greenhouse smells of plants and flowers, just like nature.

And I love it.

"Green Thumb over here is in her element," Riley says, laughing and clicking his fingers in my face to get my attention.

"Do you like gardening then, Kat?" Ves asks me, and I nod.

"My mum and I would spend hours in the garden in our tiny greenhouse. I have a great rose collection going on. Well, had..." I drift off and Riley frowns at me. I don't even notice the group has stopped, and they are silent until Thallon speaks, somehow right next to me.

"Roses are difficult to cultivate well. I'm impressed, Miss?" he asks, crossing his arms. I look up and meet his gaze, holding his stare as I answer.

"Kaitlyn Lightson, and yes, they are. I lost a few in the beginning, but it's well worth the effort for the beauty that appears," I explain. "My mum and I came up with a neat trick, but it's a secret."

Thallon seems amused by my response as Riley steps closer to me, his arm returning around my waist. "I am the gardener for the academy, and I would love an assistant with special secrets. Would you be up for the job?"

"No—" Riley tries to answer for me, but I elbow him in the ribs.

"Yes, I would love that," I reply, and Thallon smiles as Riley coughs in annoyance. "So do you have any roses here?"

"This way, Kaitlyn," he nods his head to the side, and I follow him through the plants until we get to a clearing. Right in the middle is a giant statue of three angels. They all look up at the sky, at the hole in the greenhouse above them, and at their feet is hundreds of roses of all different colours. The roses twist and climb around the bottom of their stone ropes, and it's designed so beautifully.

"I think Angel Academy just got a hell of a lot better," I say and grin at Thallon.

"Agreed," he whispers so only I can hear him before raising his voice, "Let's carry on with the tour. This way leads to the dining halls, where you can get food anytime you need, but breakfast and dinner are served to your rooms. Lunch and snacks are all that can be found in here, but they don't give out the good stuff like sweets unless there is a party."

"I don't trust him, and neither should you," Riley whispers to me, and I turn to frown at him.

"Why?" I ask, but he doesn't answer me.

We follow Thallon through the academy as he explains our new home, and Riley doesn't say another word.

I might not know Thallon, but I'm not judging him because Riley doesn't like him. Riley has never liked anyone that tried to be my friend growing up. I always worried it was because he liked me as more than a friend, but Riley promises it isn't that. He said he just wants to protect me, but when does protecting becoming smothering?

I'm sure I'm about to find out.

CHAPTER 8

After a long day of being toured around, we finally get back to our rooms. Vesnia hugs me goodbye before going into her room, and I head into mine, surprised to see several things on my bed. I shut the door behind me and sit on my bed, picking up the map first. It's a clear map of the academy and where everything is. I pick up the blue paper next and see a class schedule written on it.

Monday- Equestrian Studies / Flight Beginner Class
Tuesday- History of Angels Class / Herbology
Wednesday- Intermediate Spear Training / Gym
Thursday- Light Angel Studies
Friday- Dark Angel Studies
Sat/Sun- Study Day

What the heck is spear training? I roll my eyes at the thought of me and a sharp spear. The only thing that is going to happen there is me somehow stabbing myself by accident—or stabbing someone else. Muttering to myself, I pick up the last note, which is on top of a white cloak that is similar to the cloak I had on last night, but this one is silky and has a strange black logo on the hood. I pick the note up and turn it over.

Be outside your room at six p.m. sharp. Wear the cloak.

I REST BACK on my bed and sigh, knowing I shouldn't like Angel Academy at all, but even I have to admit this place is pretty cool for a school.

"KAT! KAT!" Vesnia's voice drifts to me, and I hazily wake up, seeing her in a white cloak, standing over me on my bed. "It's two minutes to six, and we are going to be late."

"Shit," I mutter, jumping up and picking my

cloak up. I hurry to put it on as we leave my room and rush up the stairs, where everyone else is waiting for us. For the first time, I actually look at the other students other than Riley and Vesnia. Two girls with blonde hair that is very similar stay close together, a group of about four guys are talking quietly, but the rest of the students stand on their own, looking around with distrusting eyes. I don't blame them. Riley is leaning against the wall in his white cloak, and when he looks up, we both just smile at each other.

"I'm sorry, I was a prick," he says first.

"And I'm sorry I didn't listen to you. Besties still?" I ask, and he nods as I wrap my arms around him and hug him tightly. "I know this is all stressful, but we need to stick together to make it out of this. No matter how nice this academy is, they are hiding the fact they don't care about our lives. Remember the students that didn't catch a horse?"

"I remember, and I won't ever let anyone hurt you," he firmly states.

"Same here, bestie," I whisper back.

"You guys are so sweet. Did you ever think about dating?" Vesnia asks as I let go of Riley.

"Nope, dating would be weird. Riley and I grew up together," I answer the same thing I always say to anyone that asks, and usually, Riley would agree, but he doesn't say anything. Thankfully, one of the professors I haven't seen before walks to the middle of the staircase. This teacher is much older with a withering figure, wrinkles marking her dark skin, and her grey hair looks bright in contrast.

"Hello, new students, my name is Professor Bates. I will meet you all later this week, but for now, I am to guide you to the dining hall for a special welcome dinner," she says and turns around, no doubt expecting us to follow. We head through the long corridors and through the greenhouse until we get to the dining hall. This room is just as massive as I expected it to be with several doors going off to the kitchens behind them. With deep brown walls and real wood flooring, the room looks too polished, like it's not even real. The smell of really good food finds me as I look around the dozens of white circular tables in the room. Each table has a little candle in the middle, and they are already set up with cutlery.

"Find a seat. The food will be served, and the entertainment will start soon," Professor Bates instructs.

"Entertainment?" Vesnia whispers to me as we find a nearby empty table and sit down. Riley sits on the other side of me and no one else sits with us, giving us a clear view of the stage at the front of the room. Two bright lights shine on the stage as everyone finds their seats, and silence drifts over us all. Very slowly, piano music starts to play, a deep haunting tune that takes my breath away as the curtains of the stage slowly pull back. The first person I see is Henry at the side, his hands quickly moving across the piano, expertly playing the song without missing a beat. Like he can sense me staring, he looks up and finds my gaze, holding it for a long time.

And I feel like I don't breathe. I don't exist. I am thoroughly caught in an angel's gaze.

"Aren't the dancers amazing?" Vesnia asks me, and it gives me enough strength to look away and remember that there is actually a performance going on. Five angels dance with each other using expressive hand movements as they spin around, but never once touching each other.

The dance is a game. A game spoken with more than touch, and I'm starting to think playing this kind of game with a king might get someone killed.

CHAPTER 9

"Ready for equestrian studies?" Vesnia asks as she walks into my bedroom this morning after putting her tray back in her room. I frown at myself in the mirror as I take in the skin-tight black riding pants, the thin white T-shirt and tall boots. "Okay, you look incredible! Who knew you were hiding that kind of body!"

"I wasn't hiding, I just never wear things like this," I reply.

"Want me to French plait your hair out of the way?" she asks. "And yeah, you've been hiding. Or more likely, a certain bestie was hiding you away from all the other fish in the ocean."

"Riley just sees me as a friend, Ves," I remind her as I sit on the floor in front of where she sits on my bed, and I grab a packet of Parma Violets to chew on as she does my hair. Who knows what I'm going to do when I run out of my sweets? Have a mini-breakdown maybe? She slowly brushes my hair before starting the plaits, and I try not to wince from how hard she tugs on my hair to keep the plaits tight.

"I think he is confused about you," she genuinely tells me.

"Nope, he isn't, and I'm not. Honestly, about two years ago, we came close to kissing and it repulsed us both," I say and chuckle at the memory. "I never had siblings, and he is my brother in that sense."

"Got it," she replies, but I sense she doesn't believe me. "I had a best friend like that back home, but our relationship turned into more just before I died."

"I'm sorry, that really sucks," I whisper, catching her dark eyes in the mirror on the wall.

"Yep, especially when I just came out of the closet with her and told my dad. My life was literally the best it could have been before it was just gone," she says.

"Well, I don't care, you know that, right?" I ask as she finishes tying the end of my plait up. I turn and look up at her, seeing the real worry in her gaze. "You are my friend, and I don't think anyone should have to hide who they like or love."

"I'm happy I've told you now. I spent years worrying about telling my family and friends before, and I don't want to start off my second life like that," she firmly states. "My dad told me to always be proud of who I am and who I love. I fully intend to live my life that way."

"You can tell me anything, just for the record. I won't judge you. Ever," I say and stand up. "And by the way, the riding outfit looks amazing on you too."

"Oh I know," she says and winks at me. "Now, can we discuss how jelly I am that you get to be the gardener's assistant and spend time with him?"

"Hey, I thought you liked girls," I bump her shoulder as we walk out the room, and she laughs.

"A girl can change her mind for a guy who looks like that. Well, at least for one night," she replies, and I laugh with her. She does have a point.

"I'm actually looking forward to gardening. Now, if this place had a library full of new romance books, I might not try to escape in the future," I jokingly say as we get outside and breathe in the warm air. The orb is shining bright light, and I look around for the sun, not finding it anywhere. The gardens outside the academy are just as spectacular as the greenhouse, and I know I need to have a good walk around on the weekend. As I try to remember which way the stables are, Vesnia tugs me aside just as two angels land right in front of me. If Ves didn't move me, they would have knocked me over for sure. Both of them are dark angels with bright blonde, waist-length hair, and the only difference between them is one of them has green eyes and the other blue. They are clearly twins, and they never grew out of the stage where you stop matching your clothes as kids to look cute.

"Watch out, newbies," the green-eyed girl all but hisses. Jessica lands next to her a second later, frowning at me, and I smile back.

"Annie, Bonnie, this is the girl I told you two about," Jessica announces, flipping her hair over her shoulder. "Kaitlyn Lightson." My name sounds like poison as she spits it out.

"I'm Bonnie, and this is Annie. We will be seeing you around, newbie," Bonnie declares, smacking my shoulder as she goes past. I watch them walk away, and as they get to the door and go inside, Annie turns back. "By the way, the princesses always protect the queen. You should know that before you try and take the king."

"Do you think it matters that I have zero interest in the king...wait, Henry. I'm not calling him that," I mutter, rolling my eyes. Ves sighs.

"Day one, and we already have enemies. I knew there was a reason I hated high school, and this place is like high school but with angels," she drones.

"Angel high school should come with a warning about the psychopathic blondes who roam the corridors," I whisper.

"Or hot guys," she whispers back to me, nudging her head in the direction of the trees. Right at the start of the forest is a little hut, and in front of it is a shirtless Thallon digging in the soil, covered in mud. Hot damn. Sweat drips down his impressive chest onto his six-pack and that V shape that dips into his trousers. There is a tattoo on his ribs of some kind of words, and I have to snap my jaw shut as he looks up and sees us, and he waves. I wave back and all but trip on thin air as Vesnia laughs and tugs me away before I can make more of a fool of myself. We see a few more of the students from our class as we head to the stables, which are busy as I find Riley talking to a light angel near the front. The light angel lifts his bushy eyebrows and points at me, and Riley nods when he looks back.

"Welcome, class, I do hope you had a good night's sleep. My name is Professor Nina for all those who have forgotten," she comments from the stable door. "Now in my lesson, I will teach you how to care for your horse, how to call your horse on demand and become a fighting pair." She pauses and clears her throat. "I want each of you to stand a good distance apart and use your whistle. The whistle will only work if you want your horse to come, so you must want to call your horse. Let's start."

"Good luck," I whisper to Vesnia as we walk apart. I find a clear space near the edge of the stable and pick up my necklace. I place the cold silver whistle in my mouth and close my eyes, thinking of Ayda. The second I blow the whistle, a strange hum of something shivers over my skin, and I know she heard me. I open my eyes, seeing other students blowing their whistles, but there is no sound coming out, and then I hear the horses. The sound of their wings cutting through the air can't be missed. I look up as a herd of horses fly in the air, and right in the front is Ayda. She leads the group, and they fly in circles as they land right in a line behind Ayda in front of me. I smile at her and place my hand on her head, enjoying the simple contact of her soft fur. She neighs at me, and I suspect we agree. I try to think back to riding her last and how natural it felt, even though I was just in a cloak and I'd never ridden a horse before. Let alone a flying horse.

"Very good work. Except for you, what is your name?" Professor Nina asks, and I turn to see her asking a guy with brown hair.

"Eric, but I did try—"

"I think your horse has let you go for being weak. I am sorry," she softly tells him, placing her hands on his shoulders. I scream along with my classmates as Professor Nina roughly turns Eric's head to the side, and a snap rings out in the silence. Eric's body crumbles to the floor, and Professor Nina leans down, picking up the whistle and tugging it from his body. I'm shaking as everyone is dead silent, and Professor Nina goes back to her happy smile.

"Do remember that your second life is a gift in exchange for passing The Angel Academy as a strong angel. There is no room for the weak in the world of the angels," she firmly comments, and I gulp. We are all still frozen as Thallon walks through the horses, still missing his shirt, and leans down to Eric's body. Tears form in my eyes as Thallon softly closes Eric's still open eyes before picking up his body and carrying him away. I search for Riley in the crowd and find him watching me, the same look of disgust and horror in his eyes.

"Now, we will start by getting you to place a saddle on your horse and learning the correct way to do this. We will end our lesson with a little race between each other," Professor Nina comments, and then she hums a song as she walks into the stables.

Angel Academy is deadly.

And we have to survive, no matter what.

"BRILLIANT, each of you has learnt and picked up everything I've taught you today. Next, let's get you in pairs for a race," Professor Nina cheerily comments, and I want to reply that the only reason everyone has behaved is because they are shit scared of you, but I don't, biting my tongue instead as people start to pair up. Riley and Vesnia bring their horses over to me, and I look between them awkwardly.

"Erm, why don't you two team up, and I will find someone else?" I awkwardly state.

"I will race with you, darlin'," Henry proclaims, and I turn to see him walking over to me, his majestic as fuck horse behind him. His horse is pure black with long legs, which have a bit of hair around their ankles, and a massive mane of hair that touches the ground. Next to my horse, they are literally black and white.

"Wouldn't it be a little unfair, considering you are

a year older?" Riley asks as I can't take my eyes off Henry to ask that logical question myself.

"Do you want to ask Professor Happy-to-snap-any-neck Nina?" Henry questions with a smirk. "Go ahead. It will be fucking entertaining to see her kill you."

"It's cool. You two race, and I will race Henry," I cut in before Riley actually replies to that taunt. Ves nods at me, turning her horse around, and after a few seconds of Riley glaring at Henry, and Henry smiling back, he leaves with her. I let out the breath I was holding and go to Ayda's side. Placing my foot in the stirrup, I pull myself onto her back and hold her reins close as I get comfy. Henry simply uses his wings to fly up off the ground and swing his leg over his horse.

"What's your horse's name?" I ask.

He watches me for more than a second under those dark locks of hair. "His name is Maze."

"This is Ayda," I reply. "Why did you offer to race me? Surely you have better things to do."

"Well, actually, doing you would be a better thing," he drawls, and I laugh against my better judgment.

"That isn't happening, Henry-boy," I warn him.

"Trust me, I'm no boy. Tell you what, if I win this race, you go on a date with me," he darkly suggests.

"And if I win?"

"I owe you a favour. And trust me, a favour from a king is priceless," he replies, and I don't doubt it.

"Deal," I say before I can stop myself. *Shut up, Kaitlyn.* He is clearly going to beat you, and a date with a dark angel is a bad idea.

"Gather around in a line next to your partner!" Professor Nina shouts. With a click of his tongue, Henry moves Maze, and I follow him right to the front of the line. When another guy on his horse tries to move in front of us, Henry only has to look at him, and he decides the back of the line is cool. Professor Nina smiles warmly at Henry as she stops in front of us and points off the edge of the island. "I have placed magical rings in the air, and you have to pass through each of them until you get to the end of the race on the other side of the academy. When you finish the race, you're free to undo your horse's saddle and then have the rest of the day to yourselves. We will race one at a time. Are you two ready?"

"Ready," I answer, leaning up a little and swallowing any fear I have about this.

"You know the answer, Nina," Henry replies and smirks at her. Urgh, guys suck.

"On the count of five. Five, four, three, two, one and go!" Ayda clearly has a competitive side, the same as me, as she takes off and then spreads her wings out as we get to the end of the cliff and dive off. I lean down close to her body as I blink away the tears from the cold, biting fresh air to see one of the large rings in the air. It's a glowing circle full of symbols, just hanging in the air. I grab Ayda's reins tightly as Henry simply flies through it, and we follow just after him. His horse has serious speed as we follow right behind them around the bottom of the rocky academy. I'm inches away from Henry when a gust of wind blows us both a little to the left, and I scream as I slam into some rocks, cutting all my arm and cheek. Ayda cries out, and I look at her side to see she is bleeding, but then it heals before my eyes. Henry turns around, looking back, and I nod once. I don't need his help.

"We can beat them, right, girl?" I ask Ayda, and she turns back, meeting my eyes, and I swear she all but says yes before we are flying fast after Henry, ducking around the academy and going through two more magic rings. It takes me a second to see the rings are making us head up, and we need to do something to catch up. I spot a gap in the rocks, small enough to just get through. I tug Ayda's reins to the side and force her up through the gap. We speed out of the top and spin around, heading for the circle. Ayda rushes through it a second before Henry does, and then we fly to the ground, and I grin as Henry lands next to me.

"Smart move. I'm actually impressed," Henry breathlessly states, and it's only then I see he is a little pale.

"Are you sick?" I ask, and he glares at me.

"Okay, okay, you won, no need to be a dick to me," he says with mock indignation.

"And you owe me a favour," I remind him with a wink as I get off Ayda. I flinch as I touch my cheek, feeling the shallow cuts there. I lift my arm, which is covered in blood from a leaking cut, and Henry jumps off his horse. He reaches into his horse's saddle bag and picks out a small jar of red leaves.

"Here, put a few of these in your bath, and it will help you heal," Henry tells me, dropping the jar into my hand. "And don't think it means anything, as it doesn't. I will take Ayda to remove her saddle. Bye, darlin'."

"Thank you, Henry," I say.

"The king can't let his subjects bleed out everywhere, can he?" he dryly replies as he takes Ayda's reins and leads her away.

"Maybe the king isn't such a dickhead after all!" I shout, and his laugh haunts me as I walk away. I'm still smiling as I get to my room and open the door, locking it behind me.

"Blood does suit you." Ren's voice makes me jump and nearly drop the jar of leaves. I turn to see him sitting on my bed, his arms resting behind his back, his legs crossed. His black shirt is tight against his chest, his tie hanging low, and it's messy, but it suits him.

Why am I checking out a ghost?

"I would beg to differ," I reply, placing the jar on the side. Ren's eyes focus on it as he sits up.

"Dwine leaves, a rare tree in this world. Who gave you such a gift to heal with?" he drawls.

"A guy named Henry," I reply, not knowing why I'm telling the ghost this as I pull my riding boots off. "And why are you sitting on my bed?"

"I was bored. Ghost problems and all," he replies with a cocky grin. "Tell me, Kitty Kat, have you asked any angels about vampires yet?"

"Why would I?" I reply.

"To find answers. Don't you think it's strange you haven't seen another ghost around here yet?" he questions. "I hoped just seeing me and knowing about vampires would get you to ask someone, but it seems you are smarter than I thought."

"Yes, it's strange there are no other ghosts, but I actually like it. Seeing ghosts and being the weird kid isn't fun," I tell him, and his one eyebrow raises.

"Do you help the ghosts you see?" he asks.

"Help them how exactly?" I angrily question.

"Oh, I see it now," he pauses with a knowing smile. "You are scared of your powers and of the ghosts you are blessed with seeing."

"I'm not scared; I'm talking to you, aren't I?" I snap.

"We both know I'm different and that's why you talk to me," he replies. *Asshat.*

"I talk to you because you're always in my room like the stalker ghost you are. You should leave," I suggest, trying to swallow my rising anger. If he was a real person, I'd throw something at him.

"Only if you promise to ask about vampires. What could the harm be?" he replies with a big grin. "You might want to ask what a fallen angel is. Oh, and add how you're best friends with demons while you're at it. I'm joking, of course."

"Demons are real?" I ask with wide eyes. I don't know why the idea that vampires exist doesn't freak me out, but demons? An image of a red-skinned demon with horns makes me shiver as I ignore Ren. I knock the bathroom twice to make sure Vesnia isn't in there before walking in and heading to the bath. The bathroom is super modern with an oval shaped bath on white tiles, a walk-in shower against the grey exposed stone walls, and a toilet tucked away in the corner. The one wall has a row of cabinets and two sinks with mirrors above them. I start running the bath and sit on the edge, fascinated as my blood drips one drop at a time into the water.

"How long were you a vampire? Were you born a vampire or bitten like in movies?" I enquire, knowing Ren is in the room with me without needing to look away from the water.

"Born. Vampires can be turned with a bite, but only a master vampire has that skill to turn vampires, and I was the last living master vampire in existence," he sadly tells me, his voice full of longing for something I can't imagine. "Now my race will die and disappear before long. Newly changed vampires only have a ten per cent chance of surviving when they aren't in a coven with a master vampire near. Eventually my people will give up."

"I will ask about vampires as you wish," I reply, because for some silly, deep down reason, I want to give him something. Something to think of in the loneliness of the dark he is in.

"Thank you," he whispers, his voice so close to my ear that for a moment, I think I might be able to feel his breath on my cheek, but when I turn, he is gone, and I'm left thinking about the hot vampire ghost I know is going to get me in trouble.

CHAPTER 10

"What's your favourite colour?" Ves asks me as we head through the greenhouse on our way to Tuesday lessons. History of Angels is our morning class with Master Gabriel, and in the afternoon, we have Herbology with Professor Louton. For once, I'm actually a little bit excited about our day. Thankfully, when I woke up, my wounds had all healed like they never existed in the first place. I know I have Henry to thank for that.

"Green, and not a particular shade of it. I love the green of a healthy leaf on a tree to the green of the moss it falls on," I explain to her.

"I thought you'd say violet," she says around a chuckle.

"The only thing wrong about Parma Violets is

that they aren't green," I say, and we both laugh. "What is your favourite colour?"

"Red," she mutters, lifting a strand of her curly hair and letting it bounce back into place.

"I could have guessed that. Okay, what question next?" I ask, as this was Ves's idea to get to know each other a little better.

"Which boys do you have a crush on?" she asks, and my mind betrays me by flashing images of Thallon, Henry and Ren into my head. Not that I can tell Ves that I see ghosts and have done since I was a kid. Oh, and that I'm crushing on a vampire ghost who haunts my room. Yeah, totally normal.

"Wait, you're lucky and off the hook. This is our room."

"Lucky me," I grin and push the glass door open. Master Gabriel sits at the front of the class in a leather chair, a large desk right in front of him, and it is covered in bits and bobs. Ves and I find an empty table two rows back and sit down as the rest of the students pile into the room. When all seventeen of us are in here, Master Gabriel stands up and closes his hands in front of him.

"Do any of you remember the first time you were told about angels?" he asks, and there is silence for a reply. I can't remember, but Ves puts her hand up, and Master Gabriel nods for her to talk.

"I was seven, and there was an angel statue outside our local church. I remember asking my dad what it was, and he told me angels are the protectors of us all," she quietly says. "Oh, and that they have cool wings."

"A lovely story, and I'm sure in everyone's minds, there is a similar one. Angels have been in humans' lives since the dawn of time, since their earliest memory. We are unclear where our race truly began, but it is clear we were sent here to rise above human emotions and wants in order to do the right thing," he says, folding his hands together.

"And what is the right thing?" I ask.

"To steer humanity in the direction of good and not evil, of course," he replies. "In this class, I will teach you the history of the great angels who sat in the seats you are in and walked the same corridors of this academy as you do. I will teach you their names, their actions in life, and hope that when the time comes for you to shape history, you will look back to them and make the right choice," he says and sits back down. "Now come and gather a book off my desk and start reading. We have a lot of ground to cover before we can talk of the great stories."

Each of us gets a dusty book and sits back down before we open it to find it's not in English at all.

"Master Gabriel, we don't speak Latin," Vesnia says.

"I'm well aware. The Latin translation books are at the back of the class. I suggest you get to work rather than asking me questions," Master Gabriel replies, and I all but groan as I slide out my seat.

This is going to be a long class.

"HOPEFULLY, Herbology is going to be better than that. I nearly fell asleep in my dusty book," Vesnia grumbles, wiping dust off her hoodie sleeve. "It's a good thing your sneezing kept me awake."

"I don't do dust," I mumble just before I sneeze once again. I pull out my map from my back pocket and see that Herbology is in the greenhouse with Professor Louton. Vesnia hooks my arm in hers as we head down the corridor and to the greenhouse where most of our class is already waiting with Professor Louton.

"Welcome, class, to your first Herbology lesson.

In this class, we will teach you about herbs and plants that have magical qualities such as healing humans who have been poisoned or drawing metal out of a human body. These things will be useful when you finish The Angel Academy and have to look after a human of importance," she says. "It is very important you study hard for this class, because one mix-up when making a healing lotion could result in death, and I do love for my students to try out their own work on themselves."

"That got everyone's attention," I mutter because it did, and I have no idea if she is joking or not.

"Right behind me is a plant called the Dekal," she explains waving a hand at the plant with some yellow leaves scattered between purple ones. "The yellow leaves are safe to touch, but they have no healing properties. The purple leaves are deadly to touch, but they also are a vital ingredient in a lotion I want you to make. So get one leaf each and meet me at the back of the greenhouse."

Professor Louton walks off, her black high heels clicking against the stone with every step as we all stare at each other.

"Any chance someone has gloves in their pockets?" Ves asks.

Resounding nos answer Vesnia, and then we all

stare at the plant, none of us brave enough to test the warning Professor Louton said.

"I have an idea," I mutter and take a step forward. I carefully lean into the plant and pick off a yellow leaf, and then I use the yellow leaf to very carefully pull a purple leaf off the plant. I raise an eyebrow at Vesnia who grins and goes next as I head down the path and to the back of the greenhouse. Thallon is talking quietly with Professor Louton as I get closer, and she laughs at something he said, placing her hand on his shoulder. I clear my throat to interrupt, not knowing why I felt like I had to do something to get noticed. Thallon smiles at me and then sees the leaves in my hand. He rushes over, picking a jar up off the side, and I drop the leaves in the jar.

"Are you still getting them to pick these leaves?" Thallon asks. "Last year, three students died from accidently touching them."

"And those were three students who did not deserve to be an angel," she sourly replies, her eyes locked on me.

"I figured using the yellow leaf to hold the purple was the idea," I say quietly.

"Did anyone die?" she asks, and I shake my head. "Shame, it would have been a more interesting class.

We do have all year though." Thallon gets a jar for Vesnia as she comes over with her leaf, and she places it in the jar.

"Both of you need to find the next ingredient. It's an orange herb that smells like vodka, and it grows by the trees outside. Gather a handful, won't you?" Professor Louton demands.

"Don't let the herb touch your lips. It kills if ingested," Thallon softly tells me.

"Thallon, don't you have work to do?" Professor Louton snaps.

"As always, Professor Louton," he replies and winks at me as he walks away. At least one of the angels here isn't trying to kill me.

CHAPTER 11

"Welcome to intermediate spear training. My name is Professor Badhur. In this class, we will train your bodies in the ways of angel fighting, and with weapons that are suitable. Year one is focused on spears like these." He waves a hand at the line of spears held on a stand near the wall. "And in year two, we will move on to swords, and year three is your choice. Sometimes I will teach this class and gym afterwards, and other times there will be another professor."

"Sir, but none of us knows how to fight at all," a girl points out from our class.

"Miss Pennlop, I am aware everyone in here hasn't got a clue how to use weapons, but there is something you are all forgetting," he replies and crosses his arms against his chest. "In the world of angels, your bodies are reborn, and you now have fighting skills you never did as a human. This class is simply here to guide you in what your body already knows."

"Now this is a class I'm excited for," Riley whispers to me, and I roll my eyes.

"Everyone get a spear and stand in a circle around me," Professor Badhur demands. Vesnia chooses a small black speak with silver ends, Riley gets the biggest spear he can with dragon symbols wrapped all around the white marble spear. I search through them as everyone chooses theirs until I find a deep red spear with black angel wings wrapped around it. The tip is silver and quite high with a long point. I pull it off the stand, feeling the weight, and I head back to the group, realising I'm the last one left and they are all staring at me. I slide into the space between Vesnia and Riley that they left for me and rest the spear in front of me, both my hands wrapped around it.

"Now one by one, I want you to attack me," the clearly mad professor suggests. "Mr. Becker, you may go first." Riley doesn't need asking twice and runs at the professor, swinging his spear towards his chest. In one move, the professor grabs the end of the spear, pulling it towards him and grabbing Riley's shirt. The next second, Riley is flying across the room and smacks into the wall on the other side. I take a step towards him, but the professor calls my name next, and it's a warning, without him needing to say anything, not to go after Riley. I grip my spear tighter as I step forward towards the professor, who merely smiles.

"I don't have a chance. You are a skilled fighter, so I give up," I say, and I drop the spear on the floor, watching it bounce between us for a moment until the professor claps.

"To admit defeat is a strength all to itself. Running headfirst into a battle you know you cannot win is not the way of the angels," the professor says, leaning down and picking up the spear. "Angels always, always win, and the only way to continue that in the future is to be smart, to train and become stronger than your opponent."

He hands me my spear as Riley gets back to us, his cheeks bright red, and he won't look at me. "Now each of you get in a line and follow my moves."

We line up, and for the next hour, the professor

teaches us how to hold our spears, how to attack with them and make perfect hits one after another. Eventually the professor makes us line up in teams, and I pick Riley.

"Did you know the answer and not tell me? It hurt like a bitch to get thrown across the room, Katy," Riley asks as I block his spear, clashing it against mine. I push him off and continue to circle him as the professor instructed. When he takes a next step, I slam my spear down towards him, and he pushes me off, but the tip of my spear catches his shoulder.

"I didn't know until I did it. Sorry if you hate me for that," I say.

"I don't hate you, but I don't want to fail this academy and die," Riley all but shouts, and my cheeks light up as I know everyone is staring.

"Riley, I'm not your enemy, you know that, right? This isn't a competition," I remind him.

"I know that," he softly says, his whole attitude changing as he realises he has pushed me too far. "But it's hard to share you with this academy. It just used to be us, you know?"

"In a small town with nothing to do, I remember," I say with a smile. "We could get back to that one day."

"We will always be angels, and angels don't belong in tiny towns in the Lake District," he reminds me, and I know he is right. Maybe we both need to look for a different future now.

CHAPTER 12

"Please find a seat, angels in training," Professor Nina suggests as I get to the clearing in the gardens outside. There are little cushion seats dotted all around the clearing, and I close my eyes for a second, enjoying the warm air and the feel of the light on my face. The smell of all the plants nearby makes the air sweet, and for a moment, it doesn't feel like I'm somewhere I don't want to be, it feels relaxing. I find Riley near the front, and Vesnia follows me over as we both find a cushion nearby. He looks back, smiling tightly.

"Things are still weird with you two then?" Vesnia whispers to me.

"Same as always. Since we came here, that is," I whisper back, wondering if there is some way I can fix my friendship with Riley. I know it's super complicated between us, but I'm not sure how to fix something I don't know how was broken in the first place. We can't go back to the town where it was just us, day in and day out, but surely Riley knew that. No matter what paths our future took, it would change us.

Either way, he is my best friend, and I need to figure out a way to make him happy.

Professor Nina claps her hands a few times, and we all turn to see her stood in front of four light angels. "I will be handing you over to the final year light angel students after some brief words. As you all know, this year for new angels is a choice between the light angel side of your soul and the dark angel side. These two days once a week are to help you see what comes with the choice you will make. As the light angels are going first this year, I will leave you in their hands to explain more."

Professor Nina spreads her wings wide and flies into the air, leaving us all staring in wonder until she disappears from sight.

"Right, it's always awkward to begin with, but I'm Oliver. This is Teddy, Mike and Dave," he introduces his friends, still with that overly big smile. "Light angels are the good guys, that's what you should know first. We love to heal, to be kind, we cannot lie, and we are blessed with good luck. It comes in handy when you make a partnership with a dark angel and you are given a human to look after."

"Are partnerships always between light and dark angels? Not two lights or darks?" Riley asks.

"Mr. Becker, it's an honour to meet you, and the answer to your first question is yes. They must be a balance in the human's decisions, an angel on each shoulder, if you will. Dark angels corrupt their human's souls with sin and greed, and our job is to show them light," he answers.

"Is it true that light and dark angels can't have children together or be together in any sense?" Vesnia asks.

"That is true, but it's more a choice than a rule. Light and dark angels do not make the best of friends, and that will not change in any future. When you make the choice, you will feel the differ-ence the power of an angel makes in your soul," Teddy answers her to explain.

"But enough with the depressing stuff, right?" Oliver says with a big grin that for some reason, I don't want to smile back at. "We are going to start the class with meditation and then a small demonstra-tion of your powers you could get as a light angel."

"Close your eyes and listen to the world around

you. Focus on the peace of the world," Mike says to us as all four of them sit down. I place my hands in my lap and close my eyes, listening to the sounds of everyone breathing and not liking having to sit still for this amount of time. Eventually Mike calls out that we can open our eyes, and I see Oliver standing at the front, holding a pot with a small green plant in the middle of it. Very slowly the plant grows into the air into a small tree, and dozens of long branches stretch across the sky above us. I jump when something lands in my lap, and I look down to see a small red jewel that sparkles in the light.

"A gift from us to you," Oliver says, and I look around to see everyone has a different coloured crystal in their hands. "Why don't you all come and talk to a light angel and ask any questions you wish."

Riley is up in seconds, walking over to Oliver, I suspect, and I follow him over. By the time I get through the other students, they are deep in conversation and laughing. Oliver places his hand on Riley's shoulder as I get closer.

"Hey, I'm Kaitlyn Lightson," I say, offering my hand to Oliver. He looks at it for a moment and then ignores me completely.

"Riley, I have a PlayStation 4 in my room. Want to ditch class and come play?"

"Yeah, man!" Riley all but shouts. "Later, Katy." He calls to me as they both walk away. It becomes clear to me that light angels might look all holy and perfect, but on the inside? They can be just as dark as the rest of us.

CHAPTER 13

"What the hell is that noise?" I grumble, pushing back my covers and looking at the window. It's still dark outside. I crawl out of my bed, following the sound of the thumping music to my door, and look out to see Jessica holding a stereo above her head with a line of barely dressed dark angels dancing next to her.

"Party time, bitches," Jessica shouts as Vesnia opens the door, looking as half asleep as I am. "Especially you, Lightson!" she shouts, her voice cutting through my groggy senses and waking me up. "Get dressed into something sexy, everyone!" Without even acknowledging her, I slam my door shut and instantly wish it had a lock on it as Ves walks in, looking far more awake.

"We should get dressed and see what they want. They aren't going to go away," she replies and walks to my wardrobe, tugging it open. I pull my hair up into a messy ponytail as Vesnia chucks the only dress I have at me.

"Fine," I mutter as Vesnia goes through the bathroom to her room to no doubt get ready. I pull off my pyjamas and slide into the silver dress I've never worn before. My mum bought it for me because she said it was on sale and it reminded her of me. The silver material is soft, sticking to my body almost perfectly and falling to my knees. It has a sweetheart neckline and gaps on the sides, showing off my ribs. Thankfully, it has a built-in bra, so I don't need to wear one. I slide on my socks and Doc Martens before grabbing a packet of Parma Violets.

Not bothering with knocking, I head through the bathroom and into Vesnia's room as she finishes brushing her long, kinda crazy but beautiful red hair. I pop a sweet into my mouth as I wait for her to put on her shoes, and we both head out into the corridor. Jessica and her backup angels are at the top of the stairs, and I eat another sweet for good luck as we head up to meet them. The music is still blasting loudly, and it makes me wonder if the teachers care at all. Jessica takes her time running her gaze over me, and whatever she sees, she clearly isn't impressed with.

"Finally," she overdramatically huffs and claps her hands. "The boys have already gone, but I suppose it doesn't take them long to get ready for a party."

"There's a party?" Vesnia asks with interest.

"Of course! It's the first day of seeing what dark angels really do for you guys, and hosting a party is a good way to see the action," she replies and practically bounces to the door to the corridor. We all follow her through the academy and outside towards some of the cabins on the left side I haven't been near yet. They are well hidden in the thick trees, but one of them stands out more than the others. The house is covered in angels sitting on the roof, on the porch and all over the grass outside. Fairy lights are wrapped around the thick bannisters and the edges of the roof, and the inside of the cabin has different coloured lights flashing through the glass as they move.

Vesnia hooks her arm in mine as we walk through the dark angels littering the grass, the heavy scent of alcohol filling my nose and making it twitch as we head into the cabin. Loud music blasts into me as much as the heat of the room does as we look around, and I have no clue where to glance first. The one half of the room is full of angels dancing in pairs, looking close to having sex as they enjoy the music, and the other side of the room is no better. Angels fill the sofas, practically eating each other's faces off, but it doesn't seem like they are doing more than that right now. I cough as I breathe in a mouthful of what I'm sure is weed, and I spot a few people smoking it near the entrance.

"You brought the new meat. Interesting, my queen," a dark angel with mousy brown hair says to Jessica, before tugging her away to one of the sofas.

"The light and dark angels certainly have different ways," I mutter to Vesnia as we move away from the door. Vesnia nods her head to a door at the back of the room, and we both go through it to a game room full of more dark angels. The pool table is now a drink table filled with every kind of alcoholic drink you could find. We carry on through and find the kitchen where Riley is talking with two light angels, the only light angels I've seen in here.

"There you are, we gotta go," Riley states, grabbing my hand and tugging me to his side a little too roughly.

"What's the rush?" I ask.

"Yeah, asshole. Don't you like my house or my

party?" Henry asks from somewhere very close behind me. I freeze as he places his hand on my waist and his body presses into mine, his breath moving my hair on the top of my head as Riley stares at him. For a moment, I see so much pain and anger in my best friend's eyes that I want to tell him I will leave...but Henry is right. I actually want to see what dark angels are about, and if this is their way, then for now, I will have to play by their rules.

"No, and let my best friend go," he bites out.

"What does your best friend want?" Henry sarcastically asks, clear humour in his voice, and Riley's eyes drop to mine.

I know he is going to hate me before I've even spoken. "I want to stay. I want to know what dark angels do as much as you liked learning about light angels yesterday, Riley." He stares at me in shock for a second before he changes his whole expression and drops my hand like it's on fire.

"I never had you down for one of *those* girls," he growls at me before walking away with his new light angel friends following behind him. Henry doesn't move from my back nor take his hand off my waist as I suck in a deep breath of air.

"Thank you," I say very quietly, not even wanting to hear the words myself.

"I don't like bullies," Henry whispers to me before letting me go. I turn around, but he is gone, disappearing into the crowds of people, and Ves hands me a drink.

"I knew you'd need one the moment Riley grabbed you," she explains, and I tightly smile. "Let's just have fun, yeah?"

"Why not?" I answer, and Ves laughs, pulling me through the house and into the dancers. For a few hours, I forget I'm surrounded by angels or that my best friend is mad at me, and I just dance, but in the corner of my eye, I see Henry always watching me, always letting me know I'm not alone.

"WHICH WAY IS OUR ROOM AGAIN?" Vesnia asks, and I giggle in response. I don't have a clue, the academy all looks the same to me. We stumble down a corridor and find a door at the end, which Vesnia opens up, and we peer inside. The room has mirrored walls, and in the centre is a massive black, sleek piano.

"We had a piano at home, and I always loved playing. Watch!" I say, stumbling into the room as Ves follows, giggling away. She sits on the floor by the stool as I press a few keys before I start playing my favourite song to perfection. It's not a song anyone would know because my mum said she learnt it from her mother, and her mother taught her before that. The song always spoke to me in the way that music can speak to everyone. No matter who you are in the world, good music always links us all. It shakes us to our core, making us feel emotions we haven't before, and this is why I always loved it. The end part of the song makes me pick up speed on the notes, my fingers flying across the piano faster than I ever thought I could do before. As I press the last note, I sigh, letting out the joy of the memories I have with my mum teaching me that song.

I will see my parents again. It's impossible to imagine that I won't, and I can't wait to see how happy they will be when they know I haven't died. Clapping interrupts my thoughts, and I turn to see Thallon in the doorway, a big smile on his face. I glance at Ves, only to see she is fast asleep on the floor.

"When did you learn to play like that?" Thallon asks, stepping into the room.

"Erm...I...well," I mutter.

"Sounds like erm is a good teacher," he teases,

and I blush. "But would you like me to help you carry your friend back to your room?"

"Yes, that would be great," I say, standing up and feeling a little wobbly. Thallon notices and grins as he picks up Ves and flings her over his shoulder.

"First dark angel party, I'm guessing?" he asks, and I nod. "I always loved learning about the dark angels, and trust me, there is a reason for the parties."

"I thought it was just to have fun," I say, as that's all I saw tonight.

"Then you need to look below the surface," he suggests as we walk down the corridor. The only sound is our shoes against the stone and Ves's snoring.

"Why don't you have wings? Are you human or something else?" I ask, knowing the booze in my system is making me braver than I usually am.

"I never made a choice between the light and dark fire because they both call to me. I said I would choose, but it's just never felt right over the years. Eventually, I've come to understand there must be a higher reason I can't choose, and when the time is right, the light above will show me," he beautifully says.

"It must be so beautiful to believe in something you have never seen," I whisper, but he hears me.

"You believe in love? In trust? In hate and in lust? These are things we can never see, but we know they are real. My belief in the light above and his plan for us is the same," he gently tells me.

"Then you are stuck here," I reply, crossing my arms from the chill of the academy in the middle of the night. I'm so glad I can have a lie-in tomorrow and not have to worry about waking up early for class.

"For a reason, yes. Tell me, have you figured out what you want to do with your life yet?" he asks.

"I'm eighteen and currently had a weird year, so nope," I answer, making him laugh. Gosh, he has a sexy laugh.

His lips twitch in amusement. "Thank you," he tells me, and I stare in horror as I realise I must have said the sexy laugh thing out loud. To my great relief, we get to the top of the staircase to our rooms, and Ves chooses then to wake up as Thallon carefully puts her down.

"Thank you for the lift, sexy gardener guy," she mumbles and then walks shakily down the stairs.

"I should go and make sure she gets into bed and

there is a glass of water waiting for her to wake up to," I say, and Thallon nods.

"Tomorrow I need help with the gardens. I know it's your first day off the academy, so you can say no —" he says.

"I'd love to help you. What time and where do you want to meet up?" I ask, seeing the awkward relief in his eyes.

"Meet me at ten in the morning by the roses," he tells me before he turns away and starts to walk off. "And goodnight, Miss Lightson. I hope you sleep well."

"And you, Mr. Cross," I reply as I step onto the stairs. Against my better judgement, I look back and find his eyes watching mine so closely.

Both of us smile, and I shake my head, knowing I need to get into bed. After all, I have a new job starting tomorrow.

CHAPTER 14

"Morning, sleepyhead," Ren whispers to me, and I blink my eyes open to see him lying on the bed next to me, his head resting on the other pillow yet leaving no imprint. I should be scared, but instead, I find myself just simply staring at him, wondering why he doesn't scare me one bit.

"Why don't I see other ghosts here?" I ask first, not moving as he reaches over almost like he wants to touch my cheek, but he can't.

Ghosts can't touch.

"Do you miss seeing them?" he questions me back. I take a second to actually think about it, because for the longest time, I hated my ability to see ghosts and thought it was always ruining my life. I couldn't go on holidays because being in new places meant new ghosts. I couldn't even go into the park near the woods in my town because three ghosts of children were always there and they scared me.

Everything about ghosts scared me, and now...I almost miss being something different, because my powers were the different part of my life. I felt like I had a destiny, some reason in the world for why I have these powers.

But now, in this magic world, I'm just normal.

"Yes...it always felt like seeing ghosts made me different, and now I'm just another angel in training in this academy," I admit to him.

"Whatever you are, Kaitlyn Lightson, you are not just another angel," Ren almost softly tells me before he slowly fades and leaves me alone on the bed. Whatever Ren is, he isn't just another ghost.

And I think we both know that. Rubbing my eyes, I get out of bed and have a quick shower before blow-drying my hair. I get dressed in black skinny jeans, a purple tee that says, "I'm rubber and you're glue," and my Doc Martens before eating some of the breakfast off the tray. I knock on Ves's door before going inside to see she is still fast asleep on the bed, snoring away. I decide to leave her to it and head out to meet Thallon in the greenhouse, even though I'm a little bit early. The academy is oddly silent as I walk through the halls, and I head outside this time, walking through the gardens until I get to the other side of the building. At the doors to the greenhouse, Thallon is waiting with a light angel woman with long black hair in a complicated braid. They both turn to look at me as I get closer, and the woman breaks into a big smile. She is super pretty with long eyelashes surrounding deep blue eyes, and she has a model-like body, unlike my own skinny ass. I wish I had curves like her.

"This is Kaitlyn Lightson, the girl I was telling you about," Thallon introduces me. "Kaitlyn, this is Hazel Jackman, and she is an old student who is here visiting in her time off. I was telling Hazel about your incredible piano skills as she loves to play as well."

"It is very nice to meet you! My brother is the only other person I know who can play the piano here right now. It seems like a lost art," she cheerily says and looks over my shoulder. "Oh, here is my brother now."

Without having to look behind me, I know Henry is there; his presence is like a wave washing over my body every time he is in the room. Henry stops next to me, his hand brushing mine for a brief second, and that's all it takes to make me shiver. Hazel kisses Thallon's cheek, quietly saying something as she says goodbye and goes to Henry.

"Let's go and chat up, brother. I have a lot to tell you," she says, and he smiles at her. Actually smiles, white teeth and all.

"How is your new husband? I don't have to break his face any time soon, right?" Henry asks, and Hazel rolls her eyes.

"Always so dramatic, little brother. Times were easier when you only cared about Sonic the Hedgehog games and if I ate your chocolate yoghurt," she says with a small giggle.

"I loved the old Sonic games, and of course Amy was my favourite," I say, and they both turn to look at me. I see the similarities straight away when they are next to each other. Same nose, same cheekbones and smile.

"Why? All she did was follow Sonic around," Henry asks with a frown. "At least be cool and admit you loved Tails."

"Because she loved him no matter what. It's quite romantic, and I always preferred their story over princesses' fairy tales," I say, and he smirks at me.

"It was lovely to meet you, Kaitlyn," Hazel says, tugging her brother away. "Bye, Thallon!"

"Have fun gardening," Henry says with a patronising smirk, still eyeing me curiously as he walks away with his sister.

"We will," Thallon replies and smiles down at me. "I thought we could cut some of the roses as they need tending. You can even keep some for your room if you want. I can get you a vase from the kitchens."

"I'd love that," I reply as we head into the greenhouse. The familiar smell and comforting warmth fill us as we head through the empty pathways to a small shed at the side. Thallon gets out two sheers and two pairs of gloves, which I slide on as he gets out a basket for the roses to go in.

"Tell me about yourself, what you did before here," Thallon asks as we get to the roses. "Only if you want to, that is."

"Why not?" I answer as I cut one of the red roses. "I lived in the Lake District with Riley as my best friend, and my family were well off. Which, considering the world is messed up at the moment, it gave me a good life when others don't get that."

"You are talking about the destruction of New York, London and most of southern Europe so many years ago?" he questions. "I've heard of it, but it's been a while since I've been on earth."

"Yes. It made a lot of people travel to England in hopes of work promised in the cities. London might have been gone, but gangs run the ruins there and promised anyone a job. So soon enough, people overran the country, and jobs became harder to come by. Food banks became lifelines to so many, and the rich hid in the towns far away from the cities to protect their children. It's exactly what my parents did, and yet they still lost me," I say, feeling sadness tugging at my heart.

"At least you have good memories. If it helps, your parents won't remember you. You don't just die when you become an angel, your existence on earth is gone," he gently tells me a bombshell. The rose drops from my hand, and he catches it, cutting his finger on a thorn.

"I'm so sorry," I say, taking his hand in my mine and turning it over. I press my finger on the cut and look up to find Thallon staring at me.

"I'm sorry you didn't know. They used to tell us that, but perhaps times have changed," he sadly replies.

"Thank you for telling me the truth. I feel like no one does that with me anymore," I admit.

He purses his lips, pulling his hand back and

offering me the rose. "The truth can be painful, it seems."

"So can thorns, but the rose's beauty is worth the pain."

"Kaitlyn, at least you know in your heart that your parents are happy and at peace now. They would have been lost in grief otherwise," he reminds me.

"I don't think we should be the ones to make that choice for them. If it was my child, I would want to know," I answer, and he nods in agreement. We both stay silent for a long pause before I smile at him.

"On a less depressing and heart-shattering note, what's next after the roses?"

"Hmm, we can cut some uncurable bark off the trees in the forest or de-weed the tulips near the front doors," he suggests. "New girl's choice."

"I'm going to go with the bark first," I say, and I cut another rose off, well aware of Thallon's eyes on me, staring at me like he can't figure out exactly who I am.

And at this point, neither can I.

CHAPTER 15

"My legs hurt, my arms hurt, even my brain is hurting right now!" Vesnia groans, wiping away a line of sweat from her forehead. I do the same, sucking in a deep breath after the five-mile run around the academy the "lovely" gym teacher, Professor Martin, made us do. We all thought spear class was getting easier now we know a little how to fight with the spears without hurting ourselves, but the gym has stepped up its mark.

"Looking tired, darlin'," Henry drawls from somewhere nearby, and I straighten my back, turning around just as he gets to me. "Can't handle gym?"

"I can handle it just fine," I protest, placing my

hands on my hips as Professor Martin comes over, placing a hand on Henry's shoulder.

"What can I do for you, Mr. Ravaric?"

"Professor Louton needs to see you. She asked me to watch your class for a moment seeing as I had finished my exam," Henry explains like a good dark angel, smile and all.

"Very well. Do not cause trouble, young king," Professor Martin taps Henry's shoulder a few times before walking out of the gym. Henry pulls a flask out of his jacket and walks to the benches on the other side of the room, sitting down and taking a long sip. He then lights a joint of weed, right here in front of everyone and takes a long drag. Before I think about it too much, my feet walk me straight up to him, and I pluck the joint out of his hand. Dropping it on the floor, I watch his ember eyes as I crush the joint under my shoe.

"Rude, darlin'," he mutters, leaning back on the bench behind him. I take a seat next to him, pulling my legs up to my chest and wrapping my arms around them.

"It's no good for you and illegal where I come from," I tell him.

"It's not illegal where I buy it from, so that's all

that matters," he replies. "Are you trying to save my soul, darlin'?"

"What do you think Professor Louton wanted to see Professor Martin about?" I curiously ask, ignoring his question.

"Fallen angels or at least one fallen angel they both went to the academy with," he says.

"What's a fallen angel?" I ask.

"Shit, they haven't taught you this yet? You've been here two weeks now," he mutters and rubs his eyes in clear annoyance. "Fallen angels are angels who willingly step into hell. An angel recently jumped into hell for a demon he fell in love with, and now everyone is mad."

"Whoa," I whisper.

"But the new queen of hell released all the spirits that the old king locked up in hell, and now there is a natural balance. For some reason, the angels are more scared than ever, I can sense it," he tells me.

"Is that a dark angel power?" I ask.

"Sort of. We can all sense when someone is scared," he explains. "That is an angel power."

"Why did you choose to become a dark angel?" I ask.

"Because my soul lives in the dark, and if you're

honest with yourself, Kaitlyn, you will find your soul belongs in the dark with me."

I don't move as he gets up, ditching the class he promised to look after, without looking back once.

KEEPING MY HEAD DOWN, I head through the gardens, running my fingers over some red flowers I don't know the name of. Sundays are my favourite day at the academy when the students all stay in their rooms or the dining hall, eating, the teachers are absent, and the world seems a little slower. Like it isn't trying to knock me off it with every turn it takes. I don't look up for a long time, having no clue where I'm walking until I come to a gate. I look up and see Thallon leaning against his cabin, his arms crossed over his light blue shirt and a friendly smile that's always there for me. He has some logs in his arms, and I'm guessing he came out to get them to restock his fire.

"Thallon what is a fallen angel exactly, and why is it bad to become one?" I ask. I don't know why I think he will tell me, but I do.

His eyes widen for a brief moment before he sighs and pushes the front door of his home open.

"You best come inside for that conversation, sweetheart."

He holds the door open for me as I step into his cabin, which smells of fresh laundry and the burning wood from the open fireplace tucked into the corner of the large room. Unlike Henry's house, this place has no rooms and is completely open plan other than a bathroom I can't see. One side of the room has a small kitchen with dark wood counters, a glass table for two, and a bookcase jammed with random books. In the middle of the room is a giant four-poster bed, the posts of which are hand-carved into horses that are jumping into the air. They match the gold sheets and big white faux fur blanket hanging over the bed. The fireplace has a TV hanging on the wall above it, and on either side is a beautiful painting of horses running in a field. There is a cosy leather sofa and coffee table facing the fire-place, with one glass of what looks like whiskey on a coaster on top.

"My mum always said it was terrible to ruin a table with the bottom of a glass. We had coasters everywhere around the house because my dad would constantly buy them for her when he had to travel," I say rather randomly as Thallon closes the door.

"Your parents sound very in love," he replies. "Would you like a drink?"

"Yes, they are, and I'd love a cup of tea," I say, walking into his space, noticing the piles of books on his bedside tables and a small unfinished wooden horse sculpture, and a knife next to it with some wood carvings. "Milk and one sugar please," I say to his unasked question as I choose to sit on his sofa, crossing my legs. The room is oddly silent as he makes the tea; the only sounds are the kettle boiling and the spoon hitting the cup as he mixes the tea.

"Thank you," I say, accepting the red cup, and Thallon sits down next to me, picking up his drink. I don't dare sip the tea until it's cooled down, but Thallon downs his whiskey in one go before putting the empty glass back down.

"I presume you know fallen angels are angels that went into hell and lost their wings, becoming the fallen," he asks, and I nod. I didn't know they lost their wings though. "The only angel known to make this choice was Lucifer, the previous king of hell. But recently an angel I was friends with made a choice to go into hell after his mate."

"Why would he do that?" I ask. "Losing his wings for his mate...it sounds terrible."

"At the academy, they will teach you that not

only is magic the most powerful thing in this world, but so is love. I don't know why Morgan did what he did, but I know he did it for love," he answers me. "But why do you ask about fallen angels now?"

"I heard the teachers are worried," I admit, and he frowns.

"It's not the fallen angel that has them worried, but what the balance of the souls has done to another race," he explains, though I can tell he is holding back some truth here. "Not every race in the world gets along, and any change makes ripples across the world that we all feel."

"Like a fallen angel?"

"Yes," he replies with a sad smile. We both sit in silence as I sip my hot tea, and I'm happy to report Thallon can make a damn good cup of tea.

"Do you read a lot then?" I enquire, nodding my head at the piles of books.

"Yes, but all my books are in Latin, and they are my way of finding answers about who I am and why I'm not clearly light or dark," he tells me. "So far, there isn't an answer other than someone pushing me into a choice."

"That would be horrible. I might be new to this, but I understand that everyone should have a choice," I say.

"And that's another reason I like you, Kaitlyn Lightson. You never judge me when everyone else does," he says with a grin.

I smile at him, a real smile that makes me feel safe. "You might not like me in a few hours when I raid your fridge and steal your TV to watch anything. You have no clue how much I miss Netflix and my movies."

"My home is yours," he waves a hand. "But touch my peanut butter cups, and we might have a problem."

"I promise not to touch them," I say around a giggle, and he laughs with me. Even when we just talk of war and nothing but destruction, he still is starting to feel like home.

CHAPTER 16

"When angels first arrived on earth to see humans, tell me what the first five things they saw were?" Master Gabriel asks, and I try to swallow a yawn as Miltona, the class teacher's pet, puts her hand up.

"They saw pain, lust, hate, joy and love," she sweetly answers.

Nodding, he leans against the desk, tapping a pen on his leg. "Correct, but what was the very thing they were missing?"

"I am unsure, sir," she answers, sounding panicked.

"They were missing guidance, and that is exactly what we became for them," he smoothly answers.

"Why was it our choice to guide them?" I ask.

"Surely free will is what any god wants for his child, the humans, right?"

"Who says the god who gave you a second chance at life wants humans to have free will?" he asks.

"Because they are free, and we are not," I point out.

"Very smart, Miss Lightson. Freedom has to be earnt in our angel lives, and guidance is how we slowly pay back," he replies. I tightly smile at his bullshit answer just as Ren appears on my desk. Literally sitting on my desk, his arms crossed and a playboy grin on his lips.

There are two sides to Ren. One is like this: playful, relaxed and fun. The other side, his serious side that tempts me with promises and truths, is far more alluring.

"Ask your teacher about vampires," he suggests. "You did say you would after all. Now is perfect."

"No," I hiss back, and Ves looks at me strangely from my side. I try not to look at Ren as he gets up off my desk and walks around me. His fingers play with my hair, and I can almost feel the strands moving. I can almost feel him so close to me.

"I wasn't asking, Kaitlyn Lightson. Ask away or I will be your new version of a haunted house," he threatens so sweetly. Poison wrapped in candy. That is exactly who Ren is.

"Master Gabriel, can I ask something off-topic?" I question the second he finishes his speech on the holy blessing that angels are or something. I wasn't listening thanks to my ghost vampire friend.

"I will allow it. What is your question?" he asks, and I clear my throat, finding the strength to say it.

"Are vampires real in this world?" The second he registers my question, a nervous look flickers over his features for just a second.

"Why would you ask such a thing?" he questions, and I shrug. I can hardly tell him the real reason.

"I've heard demons are real. Why not vampires?" I ask. "There are enough movies about them."

"I do not lie, and you know this well. Yes, vampires are real creatures of this world, and they are truly evil beings. Vampires are born to do one thing and only one thing. Destroy," he says, and I gulp.

"He judges us all because of what one vampire discovered," Ren says with a low laugh.

"Surely that can't be the entire race. Are you basing your opinion on one vampire's actions?" I ask.

"I do not judge entire races on the actions of one,

and it is rude to consider I do. In this world, you will find so many creatures, but a vampire will not be one, I'm afraid," he firmly states, and I want to tell him I'm looking at a vampire ghost right now.

"Why?" Vesnia cuts in, clearly interested.

"Angel blood to a vampire is more seductive than any treasure in the world. Long ago, we were at war with vampires, and we won. What is left of their race will die in time," he explains.

"Ask about born vampires," Ren pushes.

"Can they be born?" I enquire as he tries to change the subject and turns to the board. He tenses up and looks back at me.

"Not since a great mistake was made, no. Now unless your questions are about the next project, I suggest you keep them to yourself, lass," Master Gabriel states, and I nod in agreement. Ren winks at me before disappearing once again, and now I have a million questions for him. If vampires are evil, does that make Ren the same?

Why would Ren come to the angels if they were at war?

I make a mental checklist of things to ask him next as Master Gabriel asks us to get into pairs and go outside to note things of interest on the academy castle.

"Riley, can I work with you?" I ask him, hoping he will say yes. I need us to get back to some kind of normal, and we haven't had any time alone together recently. He sighs before nodding once, holding out his hand. I grip his hand as we get up and leave the room after the other students, feeling Master Gabriel's eyes on me.

"I didn't know you liked vampires, Katy," Riley says into the awkward silence drifting over us. "Or guys like Henry or Thallon, while we are on the subject."

Tugging the ends of my hair, I grab his arm and stop him in the corridor. "You will always be my best friend; you don't have to be scared of losing me."

"I'm not scared," he scoffs, tugging his arm away from me, but I see right through it and we know it.

"Why don't we ditch class and go and get snacks? We could find a tree to sit under and talk like we used to all the time?" I ask, and he runs his fingers through his hair a few times.

"Alright," he finally agrees, and I grin, hooking my arm in his. "As long as you don't spill orange juice on me like that time in middle school. It was so embarrassing to go back to school with a big orange stain all over my trousers."

"If I remember right, you poured your chocolate

milk on me as payback the next day. Chocolate milk on trousers looks way worse," I say, laughing. He laughs with me, and for a bit, it's just like the old days with Riley and me.

And I wish it could always stay like this.

CHAPTER 17

"Sneaking out of class is against the rules, Miss Lightson." I jump out of my skin as I step into my room, finding Master Gabriel standing there waiting for me. How do the stairs enchantment not work on him?

With a sheepish grin, I reply. "I'm sorry?"

"It can be our secret, Miss Lightson. Now please come with me," he asks, and I know I don't exactly have a choice. I follow him out of my room and up the stairs. We head outside the academy and right around to the back. He opens a door I've never been in before, and I follow him into a massive library. This must be the tallest room in the academy, with rows and rows of books going all the way up to the glass ceiling at the top of the room. There are no ladders or stairways to get to the top books, and everything is silver. Silver walls, silver tiles on the floor, and a chandelier hanging in the middle of the room, sparkling bright white light around the room, reflecting off its crystals. "Please wait here a second." Before I can say yes, Master Gabriel stretches out his long white wings and flies into the air. He circles around a few times before stopping at a bookshelf and taking out a heavy-looking, black leather-bound book.

Watching Master Gabriel fly down to the ground is beautiful. Angels really are beautiful, if not a wee bit deadly.

"Any answers you wish about vampires can be found in this book," he tells me and offers me the heavy book. I take the book and flip the first page open, seeing it's a book full of paintings. The first one is an image of two beautiful men in white cloaks, their hands on the pregnant stomach of a woman with long black hair on a grey stone table, her skin paler than snow.

"This is a painting of the very first vampire. It is said two gods, both male, came from the sky and kissed the belly of a young woman. They promised her a child but failed to mention the child would be forever cursed the life of a vampire," he explains to me. "The woman died in childbirth, as do all female vampires who bring life into the world."

"That's so sad," I say, running my fingers across the painting. Master Gabriel closes the book in my hands, and I hold it to my chest. I want to know more, and I'm not sure how Master Gabriel knew that, but he did.

"Much of the past of vampires, angels, demons, wolves and fairy tales are submersed in pain and misery. We must find a way to be better than those before us, to be stronger," he states. "I hope, before I die, I will find a way to make this world as I picture it when I close my eyes."

"Wolves and fairy tales?" I question with wide eyes full of shock.

"Why don't you start with one book of monsters, and we will see about the rest?" he suggests, and I grin.

"Thank you, Master Gabriel," I answer. "Can I ask why you are called a master and the other teachers professor?'

"I am one of the ten original angels who made this academy. In honour of our dedication to young angels and making the world a better place, we became masters of the angel community," he explains. "And I'm very old, lass."

That makes me laugh. "So there is a life after Angel Academy and the job we do?"

"After a certain amount of human lives you change and care for, you will be given a pass to go to the city of angels and live there in peace," he tells me. "The city of angels is more enchanting than you could ever imagine. Many who see it never wish to leave."

"The city of angels?" I ask.

"There are three levels to this world," he explains to me and pauses. "Maybe it is best I show you." With a wave of his hand, hologram images fill the middle of the library. I only wonder for a second how he is doing this until I see what the image is.

There in the middle is earth, and above it is a glowing white line, and then there are two large rocks above mountains. I know those two as the academy, but above them is the orb, and it shines light onto a city in the clouds.

"What is this white line?" I ask, wanting to step forward and touch it.

"The portal between our world and earth. If you flew through it, you would find yourself in the skies near Ireland," he tells me. I run my eyes over the images a dozen times before seeing a red line on the other side of earth and a city in the red light from the line.

"This is hell, right?" I ask. "Where the fallen angels are?"

"You are very curious, angel in training. You remind me of someone else who always asked a million questions and wanted to learn everything the world has to offer," he muses, waving a hand and making the hologram disappear.

"What was his or her name?" I ask.

"Morgan," he softly says and sighs. "I must get back now, and so should you. I hope you enjoy the book, and we will discuss it in the future."

"I'd like that," I reply as he starts to walk away, but then he stops, looking back once.

"What made you ask me about vampires?" he asks.

"I think my curiosity is rubbing off on you," I say, making him chuckle. "But it was just random."

"Nothing is random in our world, Miss Lightson, and lies are beneath you." I try to keep a neutral face as he walks out of the library, and only when the door shuts do I feel like I can breathe again.

CHAPTER 18

An ear-splitting alarm wakes me up, and I sit up as Vesnia rushes into my room only in her pyjamas, slamming the door against the wall.

"That's the alarm for an attack. I read about it," she tells me as I get out of bed, and we both freeze as we hear someone nearby scream.

"We should go and help. Or something," I say, thinking about Riley. I can't leave him alone out there, and he would do the same for me. I chuck on a hoodie and my boots, then run out of the room with Vesnia following behind me. The corridor is jam-packed full of girls all rushing around, but none of them are getting brave enough to head up the stairs. Knowing Riley might be looking for me, I rush up the steps, Vesnia holding my hand for support. I hold in a scream when I see three bodies on the floor, all with holes in their chests near their hearts. I flick my eyes to Vesnia as a clicking noise catches our attention. We look down just as a metal gate snaps across the top of the stairs to the bedrooms, and the bars start to glow blue.

"I think we're locked out," Vesnia all but cries in panic.

"We should hide; Riley will be safe. This was a stupid idea," I mutter, looking around us.

"You could say that again, angel blood," a woman sarcastically drawls. I turn around, keeping Vesnia behind me as three women walk into the room, all dressed in leather, blood pouring from their mouths and down their necks. Even then, they are ridiculously beautiful and enchanting, and it doesn't take a genius to work out they are vampires.

"You two take the redhead. I want the blonde to myself," the vampire woman clearly in charge states. In the blink of an eye, the two other vampires are behind me and dragging Vesnia away. I scream and try to grab her foot, but someone pulls my hair, and I go flying across the room. The air is sucked out of my lungs as I smack onto the floor, and I swear I see stars. The blonde vampire is leaning over me as everything comes into focus, and she smiles.

"I might keep you as a pet. Would you like to be my pet, angel blood?" she asks, leaning down, and I hate that she smells amazing. Everything about her makes you want to go closer, even as she drips someone else's blood from her lips. "You would, wouldn't you?"

"No, you stupid bitch!" I shout at her and wrap my hands around her throat, squeezing as tightly as I can. My body buckles after she lifts a hand and slaps me hard around the face. My hands fall away from her neck as tears fill the corner of my eyes, and her hand presses my cheek against the tile. In the distance, I hear Vesnia's screams, her pleas for anyone to help her, and I want to help.

But I can't. The vampire's sickly breath blows against my neck as more tears fall, and I close my eyes, blocking out the world. If I'm going to die, it's going to be while I'm in my own imagination and in my world back home. With my family.

Suddenly her hand is ripped away from me along with her body, and I look up as Henry offers me a hand. In his other hand lies a sword covered in blood, and splatters of blood cover his white pyjama shirt. Dirt and more blood are brushed against his cheeks, and his black hair is all over the place like he just woke up.

And he is my saviour.

My hand slides into his, and he lifts me up, pulling me against his chest.

"Are you okay?" he asks me, searching my eyes for some answer he can't ask me for.

"Vesnia!" I shout as I snap out of the haze and find her on the floor, two dead vampires at her side. I search for the vampire who hurt me as I run over, but we are alone. Vesnia has two bite marks on the side of her neck, cuts all down the middle of her pyjamas, and bruises all up her cheeks.

She looks terrible, but the rise and fall of her chest gives me hope.

"We need to get her to a doctor!" I shout.

"You mean an angel healer, darlin'," he corrects me and slides his arms underneath Vesnia and picks her up gently. "Hold my sword. I think the fight is nearly over, but it's not safe for me to walk there. I need to fly her to the healer right now."

"I will fight and protect Kaitlyn here," Thallon says, and we both turn to see him walk in the room with two swords in his hands. "Go!"

"You best protect her like she is your fucking queen, Thallon. I will be back," Henry growls and takes off, flying through the door. Thallon runs to me, dropping his swords onto the floor, and then he kisses me.

His hands cover my cheeks as his lips move across mine, softly, gently and perfectly all at the same time.

My first real kiss is in a room full of dead vampires, with a bloody sword in my hand, and yet it's everything perfect with the world because it's with Thallon.

"I thought you...and shit, when I saw you covered in blood and hurt... I'm sorry if I crossed a line," he mutters, shaking his head.

"No line crossed," I say softly against his lips, even as my cheek stings.

"Good, because I want to cross this line again and again," he whispers to me, and my cheeks light up. I smile so widely until I flinch from the pain, and he gently lowers his hand to have a look. Suddenly the alarm stops, and we both breathe out a sigh of relief.

"Let's go carefully to the healers' rooms," he suggests, letting me go, and picks up his swords. "Just in case of any more surprises."

"I don't know, I like your surprises, Thallon," I reply, and he chuckles as we go to find Vesnia, and I pray she is going to be alright.

CHAPTER 19

Holding Vesnia's hand, I rest my head on her bed as I wait for her to wake up. The healers spent thirty minutes with her, using their powers to heal her the best they could. Anything else, they said, would just need rest, and her own room is best for that. After changing into leggings and a pale blue oversized shirt, I checked in with Riley, who had stayed in his room the whole time and is fine. Henry and Thallon made me hold an ice pack to my cheek for a bit, but it doesn't hurt anymore. I stare at Vesnia a little longer and look around the silent bedroom.

"Ren, are you here?" I ask into the silence.

"Who is Ren?" Vesnia asks with a little groan, and I shoot my gaze back to her as she sits up on the bed and stretches her arms out.

"My neck feels like it's been used as a dog chew toy," she mumbles, touching her neck where it is bandaged up. "Remind me never to play with vampires again."

"I'm so sorry I couldn't stop them. How are you feeling?" I ask.

"Sore and in real need of some snacks. Oh, and some chocolate milk," she says, resting back on her pillows.

"And as your non-bitten temporary slave, I'm on it. The healer demanded bed rest for you, so you will be happy to know you'll miss class tomorrow," I tell her, and she laughs before flinching.

"Really?" her eyes light up, and I can't help but chuckle. I slide my boots on and wave goodbye as I leave her room. The academy is silent after the attack, and I didn't expect it to be anything different after I saw the actual state of it as Thallon walked me to the healers. I saw dozens, if not a hundred bodies in every room of the academy, and the teachers were making quick work of dragging them away. It's not a sight I ever thought I'd be okay with seeing, but since becoming an angel, I've become numb to death, or at least since I saw those dead angels on the mountains. I go through the greenhouse and into the corridor for the dining hall when I hear shouting.

"It's madness to keep him here! We should just kill him!" Master Gabriel shouts in pure anger, and I've never heard him like that before. I pause outside the door I've just passed, hearing more talking inside, but I can't understand them from here.

Curiosity killed the cat. But luckily, I'm not a cat. Or at least that's my excuse as I push the door slowly open and sneak inside the corridor I find. The corridor turns off into two staircases, and the walls are lined with white pillars with deep shadows in between them. I carefully walk down the tiles, hearing the voices getting louder with every step, and there is a manly sounding groan. A pain-filled groan. I freeze, knowing I should go back, but I don't as I rush to the steps and slowly walk up to them. My footsteps are lost in the sounds of the pain-filled noises and Professor Badhur's demanding voice.

"Tell us how you made a group and got into the academy?" Professor Badhur asks as I get to the top of the staircase, and a hand wraps around my mouth at the same time another hand roughly pulls me between two pillars. Henry's eyes stare into mine as he lowers his hand, our bodies pressed so closely together.

I want to tell him thank you and ask why he is sneaking around too. But I stay quiet and turn to look at the room I've just walked into, trying to ignore how good Henry's body feels pressed against mine.

In the centre of the room is a man on the floor, his ankles and wrists wrapped tightly in silver chains, which are attached to the stone ground under him. The man tied up is a vampire with blood coating what is left of his clothes and his teeth bared as he hisses. Professor Badhur lifts a silver cast whip and lashes it swiftly down on the vampire's stomach.

"Tell us what we want to know, and you will be able to leave," he shouts.

"Never," the vampire hisses. Professor Louton comes into the light, leaning down and tilting her head to the side before looking to Professor Gabriel.

"We have been here for hours, as I told you when you just arrived, and nothing has changed. The vampire will not speak," she states.

"Is there any possibility of a master vampire being around?" Master Gabriel asks. "We believed all the bloodlines were killed off and what is left of the coven are mated to humans and living normal lives."

"Vampires don't ever work together unless there

is a master vampire around. That's why all the attacks on the wolf packs, the demon academy on earth, and the tales island are so concerning. We assumed we are safe, but if there is a single chance a master vampire is still alive, we must summon the angel army and find the creature," Professor Badhur says.

"Thankfully we haven't suffered as many injuries as the other races. We must be far more prepared in case this happens again. I am suggesting the angel guard be placed around the academy," Professor Louton says.

"No, the angel city has its own problems of late, but some angel guards at the academy would not be a bad thing," Master Gabriel says with a long sigh.

"Fine. I will start ripping the vampire's limbs off and see if he will talk. Or he will die, one or the other is acceptable at this point," Professor Louton calmly suggests.

"Every angel will fall under his rule. His new queen is born, and the gods will bring death to all those who seek revenge!" the vampire screams, and suddenly Ren is next to him, reaching a hand into his chest. He harshly turns his hand to the side, and the vampire screams and screams before his head rolls to the side and blood pours from his mouth.

Disgust and shock fill me as I stare at Ren, my vampire ghost, being a monster.

I guess I always knew he was a monster, and I just chose to ignore it. I chose to let him get close and to not care about the dangers. Ren turns to me, and he simply winks before fading away as the teachers all stare at the body in shock.

"Hold on," Henry whispers in my ear, holding me tight against his body. In seconds his wings surround us, and the world is dipped into pure darkness. When a trickle of light flickers in my eyes, I look up and get locked in Henry's deep gaze. Sometimes it's like the embers in his eyes bounce around, sucking you in, making you want to walk through the fire.

It's a game, and Henry is always winning.

He is the king of Angel Academy, and there is nothing the king doesn't get.

"Why were you there?"

His breath blows against my lips in the cold darkness. I don't know how he is doing this. "We all have our secrets, don't we, darlin'?"

"I have a feeling you have far more than I ever could."

His thumb lifts up, brushing ever so softly against my bottom lip. "You should forget everything you just saw. It's not good for you to know anything."

"Do you have something to do with the vampire attack?"

"Why would I?" he pulls away from me, and I suddenly realise we are in the academy gardens.

"Why didn't you kill the vampire that was on top of me?" I ask him as he walks away from me, suspicion high in my voice. "You killed the other two but not her. Why would she run away and not attack you? How did you move us here?"

"Be careful not to accuse the king who just saved your life," he coldly warns me, and without another word, he flies into the air.

CHAPTER 20

I raise my arms in the air, feeling the heat from the angels dancing around me, the loud music blocking out all of my senses I no longer want to feel. It's been a week since I saw that vampire die, and Ren hasn't appeared once. I want to ask him a million questions, and a stupid part of me might even miss him a little bit.

Partying with dark angels might not be the best way to get Henry to tell me all his secrets, but it is sure a good step in the right direction of getting his attention.

It's been a week since the vampire attacks and one awkward assembly later where Master Gabriel told us all it was a misunderstanding, and now new angel guards are flying around the academy night and day. In my borrowed purple mini dress that Vesnia let me wear, I move my hips and enjoy the music for a long moment. I feel myself relaxing and forgetting the goal, as the more I dance, the more I lose myself in the music around me.

"That's enough of the show," Henry growls in my ear, his arm hooking tightly around my waist, and the next thing I know, he is pulling me out of the room and down the corridor. We get to the stairs, and he drags me up them and pulls a key out of his pocket when we get to the top, never letting me go. He unlocks the door in front of us, pushes it open, and then drags me inside.

He flips the light switch on as I take in what is clearly his bedroom. A messy double bed is pushed against one wall with at least three deep midnight blue blankets piled on top and dozens of pillows. There are three cabinets, no doubt full of clothes, and on top of them is a mixture of books. One has five snow globes on top of it, and I walk over, forgetting the rest of the room as I stare at the globes. There is one with a yellow heart crystal inside, another with what looks like New York, and the biggest snow globe has a Christmas tree and presents in it, but it's the last one that is the best.

Inside the last one is a carousel with red horses on it, reminding me of my eighth birthday.

"One year the fair got stuck in our town for an extra few days due to a snowstorm. My mum and dad had said I couldn't go; they didn't like things like the fair. They said it was tacky, but I didn't believe them, and thankfully neither did Riley. He helped me climb out of my window, and we walked three miles to the fair. When we got there, the only ride still open was the carousel, and we rode it once before my parents caught up with us," I chuckle, remembering how mad they were. "I was grounded for two weeks, and Riley was banned from my home for a month. Totally worth it though."

"You really do see him as your best friend," Henry murmurs as he sits on his bed, stretching his legs out and crossing his arms. "And not as the boy in love with you and who is a jealous fuck."

"It's just teenage hormones, and all this change is making him cling to the past. He is still my best friend, and that's all he will ever be," I reply.

"Good, because he could never be enough for someone like you," he warns.

"And what is that meant to mean?"

"Beautiful, smart, secretive and lost. So fucking

lost," he softly tells me, tilting his head to the side. "And trust me, baby, a boy like that isn't going to save you. He will ruin you and walk away."

My breaths seem to come out laboured as I watch Henry so carefully. "What if I wanted someone else to ruin me?"

"Careful what you wish for, Kaitlyn," he warns, his eyes locked with mine as he smoothly stands up and slowly walks right up to me. I'm sure for a second that he is going to kiss me, but he walks by me and opens his door. "Now go back to your room, and don't come to my parties in dresses like that again. The dumbasses downstairs don't need a reason to do something stupid."

"At least you're admitting you're a dumbass," I seethe, pushing past him and feeling my cheeks burning red. Liking me is really that bad? Bad enough to be considered a stupid decision? Am I really that bad, that unattractive to him?

"Where you going, newbie?" the "lovely" Jessica drawls, grabbing my arm as I pass her by the front door. "Is the king bored with fucking you yet?"

"As he did with you, you mean?" I suggest, and I know I've hit a nerve as her eyes burn with anger and she shoves me against the front door, pushing her arm against my throat.

"Henry and I are long term, even when we have breaks to fuck toys like you," she sneers, leaning in closer. "And that's all you are, a toy with pretty baby eyes and tuggable blonde hair. I've let you off for now, but this is your first official warning. Back. The. Fuck. Off. My. King."

I simply smile, even as I struggle with what emotions I'm feeling inside. Henry isn't mine, and I may like him, but I doubt he likes me. I think he just finds it fun to mess with my emotions like a toy.

Just like Jessica claims.

Jessica moves her arm away when she can see she has won, and I never had to speak a word. I run off the porch and keep walking and walking until I find myself outside Thallon's cabin.

I shouldn't be here.

But why when I run, do I find myself going to Thallon?

Without thinking about it too much, I force my shaky legs to the front door and knock two times, waiting for him to answer. No one comes to the door, and I sigh, knowing I should just go back to my room. I turn around just as the door is pulled open, and I turn back to see Thallon in just a low pair of joggers, a shirt in his hand, and his hair is wet, dripping onto his chest. My traitorous eyes follow one drop that slides down a firm peck and further onto his flat, toned stomach before disappearing into his joggers. I gulp and look up, knowing I need to say something.

Anything.

"I need a friend, and you're the only one I seem to run to. I don't know why that is, but—"

"You don't need to explain yourself," he stops me and stands back, waving a hand at his cabin. "I'm never going to turn you away, so run, jog or walk to me whenever you want."

Knowing I'm blushing as that was seriously romantic, I try humour to distract myself. "Is your door open to everyone? Even Master Gabriel?" I chuckle. "I can just imagine you and Master Gabriel having a Netflix and chill night."

"I'm not sure Master Gabriel is aware of what movies are," he says around a chuckle as he tugs his shirt on and steps closer to me. "Sorry I took so long, I was in the shower."

"I could have guessed," I say, reaching up and brushing my fingers through his wet hair. I pause as he looks down at me, his eyes searching mine for permission. I lean up and brush my lips across his, softly to start with, and then I find myself searching for more. His hands grip my hips and pull me harder against his body as he deepens the kiss. I almost whimper when he pulls back and rests his forehead against mine.

"You need a friend tonight, not whatever this is becoming," he softly tells me.

"I don't know what this is either," I admit.

"We will figure it out, but I'm going to be your friend first tonight. Want a drink and some pasta? I've just cooked some, and it's warm in the pot," he asks.

"I wondered what smelt nice," I answer, stepping away. "I'd love some, thank you." He kisses my forehead once before heading to the kitchen, and I look at the window for a brief second. I'm sure I see Riley outside, but when I blink, it's just the trees, and I swear I'm going crazy.

Maybe that's exactly what The Angel Academy does to people.

And their love life, it seems.

Angel help me as I don't have a clue what I'm doing.

"Ayda, do you know all the answers that boys hold?" I ask her, and she neighs at me as I continue brushing her hair. Vesnia pops her head over the stable door.

"I guessed I would find you in here. Wanna go for a ride?"

"Where is Professor Nina?" I ask. "Only she asked me to brush the hair of every horse in here, as she thinks riding is pointless for me anymore." Not that I know what that means. Ayda and I can ride super-fast, and we have been around every bit of the academy. It's still hard to understand the bond between Ayda and me, but I kinda like to think she is my friend.

"Half the class have the same orders. I think she is just being lazy," she whispers to me. "Now come for a ride!"

"Alright," I say, and Vesnia winks at me before going off to get her horse, Teagan, ready. After sorting out Ayda's saddle and reins, I head outside and into the courtyard as I wait for Vesnia to come out. Hearing strange noises, I walk around the back of the stables to see Riley and a light angel kissing against the back of the wall. As they start tugging at clothes, I back away, and as I come back, Vesnia is there, already on Teagan.

"Why do you look angry?" she asks.

"Let's fly, and I will explain," I reply, jumping onto Ayda's back. Ayda neighs once before running off through the trees and to the back of the cliff where she jumps off. I used to be scared of this fall, but now I just love the feel of the air against my cheeks until she straightens up and glides across the air. We fly around for a good hour before Vesnia whistles and points at a patch of grass on the other side of the forest by the academy. We both land and tie the horses up before sitting on the edge of the cliff, watching the thick clouds pass by.

"Riley was kissing a girl behind the stables," I tell her. "And still he acts like I'm doing something wrong by liking other guys."

"I think Riley is clinging onto you because you are the only bit of home he has here. I'd do the same, but maybe not as bad," she suggests, and I think about it for a moment. Even if what Vesnia suspects is true, he still needs to stop acting like I'm his childhood toy that he doesn't want to give away. I've never been his, and I never will be, I'm sure of that. I knew deep in my heart as I saw him kissing that light angel...because I felt nothing, nothing like jealousy or heartbreak.

If I saw Henry, Thallon or even Ren the ghost kissing someone...I don't know how I would feel.

Okay, I do.

Murderous.

I clear my throat, trying to distract myself. "What is your home like?"

"We had a small two-bedroomed house, and everyone knew everyone else in our town. I actually loved my upbringing," she tells me. "I miss pizza though. We used to handmake it every weekend and have a family board game night."

"I can play board games, and we could sneak into the kitchens to find stuff to make a pizza on Sunday. No one is in there then," I suggest, wanting to make her feel more at home than I can tell she isn't feeling right now. It might not be much, but it will be fun.

"Where are we going to get board games though?" she asks with a big smile that lights up her whole face.

Thinking back to the board games I saw in Thallon's house, I smile. "I know just the place and a third player while we are at it."

"Another boy?" she asks, and as I nod, we both laugh. I rest my head on Vesnia's shoulder, and she whispers to me.

"Thank you for being my family when I needed it more than I realised."

I smile, knowing Ves is slowly becoming part of my family anyway. I couldn't imagine my life without my crazy red-haired friend. "Always."

CHAPTER 21

Tugging the heavy book into my lap, I rest back against the bark of a tall tree in the academy gardens. I have to pull my knees up to hold the weight of the book as I turn the page over from the pregnant woman to the next image. This is one of an almost naked man sitting on a throne with three women on their knees in front of him. Each of the women has different coloured, long dresses on, but the interesting part is how they all have their heads tilted to the side, and on their neck is a bite mark that drips blood down in a line to their chests. Each of the women is extremely beautiful and different from each other. I glance back to the man in his throne, no crown to be seen to name him a king. I turn over the next page, hearing the wind picking up speed as it blows my blonde hair off my own neck.

The next painting makes me nearly drop the book in horror. The floor of the room is made of bodies and blood, littered together until you can't see the floor. Broken parts of the wall behind them hang in tatters, and right in the middle of the ruined, death-filled room is two people kissing. The man is the same one as the previous image, but the woman is new. She has fiery red hair and a very naked body that is covered in blood as much as the man's clothes are. They kiss like there aren't bodies all around them, like there isn't pain or death.

It's just them, screw the fallen world.

"What are you reading, Katy?" Riley asks, dropping down next to me. I slam the book shut and smile at him.

"Nothing interesting," I harshly answer. I'm still pretty pissed at him.

"More secrets, huh? Do your new friends know about your ghost seeing skills?" he asks, and it almost seems a cruel question. Like they couldn't be my friends if they didn't know my biggest secret, and that's not the case.

"No one but you, and you know that. I don't think The Angel Academy wants a ghost seeing angel," I admit, feeling a little more than on edge with how he looks at me. A little part of me wishes Riley didn't know at this point.

"Have you had any trouble with ghosts here?" he asks, eyeing the book, and I cover it the best I can with my arms.

"Nope, this place is clear," I say, leaving out any mention of Ren, who has all but disappeared recently anyway. That should be seen as a good thing, considering he can apparently kill people, but damn do I miss him.

"What do you remember about the crash?" he asks, and I pause. We haven't talked about the crash at all, and I'm not sure how to bring up how sorry I am that it happened. I was driving, so it was my fault for looking away, even for a second. I know the angels say the crash was predestined and so was everyone else's accidents, but maybe I could have saved us if I were looking.

I don't remember a lot, just fragments of flash-backs that don't add up to a real picture in my mind.

"I was driving us home from the cinema, and then..." I stop, shaking my head before frowning at Riley. "I'm sorry I crashed the car because I wasn't looking. Why does it matter what I remember, anyhow?"

"I remember a man in the road," he slowly tells me. "And I don't blame you. I know it was someone else's fault, and I think that's someone we know."

"I-I don't remember that," I whisper, wondering where he is going with this. A part of me is happy he doesn't blame me, but not so happy if he is blaming some random person. There was no way an angel was in the road; I would have seen a man or woman with wings. The big wings are hard to miss.

"See, that man looked just like the gardener. The one you keep talking to," he warns me. "The one you are *far* too close to."

"That's impossible. He lives here, and he hasn't chosen a side, so he doesn't leave the academy. Ever," I remind him, feeling angry and defensive of Thallon. After all, Thallon has been nothing but good to me.

He drops his hand on my shoulder. "Something is wrong about him, Katy. Don't you see it?"

"No, I only see someone who needs to find better things to do than follow me around. Riley, for the love of god, find a girlfriend here and remember I'm your best friend," I tell him, picking up my book and walking away before he can say anything else to ruin our friendship.

"WHOA, careful with the weeds. You might pull out the actual plant," Thallon suggests, and I pause, knowing he is right.

"Sorry." I carry on my work until Thallon's hand covers mine.

I look up, and his worried eyes meet mine. "What is it?"

"It's been a hard week. Riley is acting less like my best friend and more like a jealous ex-boyfriend, and I don't see him like that. Then I ran out of Parma Violet sweets, my Doc Martens are getting grubby and need replacing, and I'm sure I'm failing equestrian studies, because I get the feeling Ayda doesn't like me."

"I'm going to need to slow that down," he chuckles, pulling off his gloves. "So no more sweets, and that makes you mad because?"

"They are my favourites," I answer.

"Okay, well, we could look in the kitchens for some," he suggests, trying to make me feel better, but that just makes it worse.

I sigh. "I already did, and they don't."

"I'm sorry," he tells me. "Now, about Riley, he will

move on. Just give him time, and Ayda does love you, how couldn't she?"

"You're right, it's just been a bad week," I say, and he smiles at me.

"We all have those," he mutters, running a hand through his hair.

"Tell me about your life before here. If you don't mind," I ask. "I need a distraction."

"Alright," he agrees, crossing his arms and looking out the window of the greenhouse. "I was training to be a pilot, just like my father was. My mum was a gardener, but she died from cancer when I was fifteen, and so I took over her gardens. It's where I got my love of gardening from. I died a week before my twentieth birthday when a plane exploded as I walked past it." He stops, and I place my hand on his arm. "Coming to the academy was not what I expected, and I wanted to go home. Eventually I realised I couldn't and found friends here, but they have all passed the academy or left. When it came to the end of my final year, I was already spending my spare time looking after the gardens, they were a weed-filled mess before, and Master Gabriel offered me the job of gardener. So here we are."

"So you can't go back to earth?"

He shakes his head. "I'm immortal and lost in a battle of choice. My place is here, and I feel that in my soul."

"Thallon, what do you miss most about earth?"

He chuckles, leaning back. "Flying a plane, oddly enough."

"I think you were always meant to be flying but not with a plane. With your wings," I tell him, and he grins at me.

"You have me all figured out, Miss Lightson."

I lower my hand as I chuckle, but he catches it, kissing the tips of my fingers. "I love your laugh."

"Thallon..." I whisper.

"I know we practically just met, and I might not know what angel I want to be, but I know who I want, and that won't change. We can take it slow, but give me a chance."

"I've never dated anyone before," I warn him. "And how Riley is acting, I don't think I should right now. Plus, I'm practically on a knife's edge at this academy."

"Me neither, but I think we can have some kind of agreement with calling it a name if you want." I can tell he is being honest, and I nod. He leans closer, brushing his lips against mine before pulling back. "Now I know why you always smell of something sweet. The Parma Violets."

I pull a mocking sad face at him. "Don't say their names, they are all gone." We both laugh as we get back to gardening. We both have something new to be happy about this week after all.

CHAPTER 22

"I get that dark angels love to party, but how does that have to do with actually being a dark angel?" Vesnia questions a guy called Tuke who's a friend of Henry's, or at least I've seen them talking together, which accounts for some kind of friendship for Henry. I've watched him around the academy these past few weeks, and I know he doesn't let anyone close, not even Jessica, who follows him like a puppy, yapping to get his attention.

"It's not to give you information on dark angels, but to see who leaves the party and who figures out the truth behind the party," Tuke comments before taking a deep inhale of his weed-filled roll-up. We aren't going to get answers from the drunk or drugged angels, that's for sure. I still keep looking around the room for Henry, but instead, I end up finding Jessica's eyes staring right back at me.

"Riddles are for losers," Vesnia mutters and rolls her eyes as Tuke wanders off to no doubt find more drugs or booze.

"Only losers who can't figure them out think that," Jessica drawls, and I tense up. Turning around, I almost scream as ice cold beer pours down my face, into my hair, and down my chest and dress. "Whoops. I'm so clumsy these days. You must forgive me."

"Forgive this, bitch!" Vesnia shouts before tackling Jessica to the floor, and I can't help but laugh. The angels form a circle around them as they fight, and I'm super impressed by how quick Vesnia pulls a chunk of Jessica's hair out. I wonder if I should help or stop this as Tuke and Henry appear out of nowhere and split them up. Vesnia is still screaming at Jessica as Tuke drags her out of the party, and Henry leaves Jessica on the floor, crying over her cut lip and missing hair as he steps in front of me.

"Hey, trouble." He sighs, and I grin. "I have a shower and answers, if you want them."

"NO! Don't tell her anything!" Jessica pleads, crawling up off the floor, and I nod once, letting Henry know I'm coming with him. Henry looks back once, and whatever is on his face makes Jessica stop, tears falling from her eyes. Without another word, Henry takes my hand in his and leads me through the party and to his room. Once we are inside, he shows me his bathroom and where the towels are.

"I have a top and shorts you can borrow if you want?" he asks, opening his chest of drawers. "Better than walking back to the academy in a beer-covered dress."

I tilt my head to the side, running my gaze over his black knee-length shorts and white tee that fits him too well, showing off all his muscles. His hair looks wilder every day I see him at the moment, but his skin looks pale. His eyes have bags under them, and I wonder how well he is sleeping.

What is wrong with my dark angel? "You could always take me back using that shadow thing you did. Is that a power all dark angels have?"

"No, and I'd rather you didn't talk about my gift," he says, handing me a pile of clothes and not meeting my eyes. "I never should have shown you what I can do."

"I won't tell, because I have my own secrets and I know how to keep them," I tell him, feeling my heart beating fast in my chest. I don't tell anyone about my secrets, especially not a boy who won't tell me any of his.

"That's the *only* reason you're still alive," he cruelly says, and I wish he was smiling as he said it. Only he wasn't, and I don't doubt he is telling me the truth. Without trusting myself not to say another word, I head into his bathroom. After quickly stripping out the sticky clothes, I fold them and leave them on the toilet. I carefully shower off and wash my beer smelling hair with Henry's shampoo and then dry off. I slide on Henry's shirt which falls to my knees and smells way too much like Henry, and I damn well like it. The shorts are a little loose, but once I've pulled the strings tighter, they manage to stay up. I run my fingers through my damp hair and stare at myself in the mirror for a second, wondering what I should do next. I look down at the small bin in the room and see dozens of blood covered tissues. Maybe he has a problem with nose bleeds?

Aren't angels meant to be immortal and never get sick?

"What are dark angels' powers then?" I ask as I walk out of the bathroom, and Henry doesn't look up from a big book on his lap. I wonder if his dark angel powers can make him sick somehow, and that's what's going on. Not that I've seen any other sick angels around now I think about it.

And Henry does seem to hide from the world all of the time.

"Haven't you figured it out yet?"

"No," I mutter in annoyance. I pride myself on being smart, and yet somehow I can't figure what the parties are all about. Ves and I have searched all the rooms we can, questioned all the angels that would talk to us, and yet we don't see a clear answer. Even then, I prefer dark angel study days to the light angel ones. All we do in that class is meditate, learn hymns and songs about good shit. One day, we even baked cookies to send to earth.

I mean, I'm all for good vibes and karma, but there has to be more to angels.

"Why do dark angels have parties?" he asks me, closing the book and finally looking up at me. I can't read his ember-filled eyes, even as I want to keep staring. "It's this simple. Dark angels need to have fun, to party, to lose themselves in something to escape the darkness they willingly walked into. The darkness gives us heightened abilities in the ways of strength, power, speed and in return, we agree to accept who we are now."

"A dark angel..."

"Darlin', I knew from the second I saw you that you'd choose to become a dark angel like me. When they take you to the ceremony room, the darkness is going to call you to it like a moth to a flame," he warns me. "And then, when you're like me, finally you will understand why I keep you at a distance. You deserve better than me, and that's why I ignore how you stare." I blush but hear his next softly spoken words. "I ignore how I stare right back at you with the same thoughts."

Crossing my arms, I watch him get off the bed and walk to me. "And why does that make you mad?" I ask.

"Everything makes me mad, angry, jealous, possessive and cruel. Darker emotions are our price as much as not being able to lie is a light angel's price."

I suck in a deep breath as the room feels flooded with tension and missing air. "All those emotions are normal for a human."

"But a human can turn them off with a flip of a switch. I will never be able to do that," he warns me, and now he is so close that our noses are touching. "You should leave."

"I should," I totally agree, but my feet stay firmly placed on the floor.

"Dark angels are seductive, but you already know that, don't you?"

My lips tilt up, and his eyes track the movement like a hawk tracks its prey. "Is this your way of asking if I like you, Henry-boy?"

"Fuck it," he growls before he kisses me. His lips press against mine with an urgency I didn't know I could feel through a kiss, but now I do. He deepens the kiss with his tongue as his hands slide under my ass and lift me up. My legs wrap around his waist on instinct as I dive my hands into his hair, moaning at how good our bodies feel pressed together.

The door slams open, and I pull away from Henry to see Riley standing in the doorframe, his eyes like molten lava and heartbreak all in one. Dammit. Henry lets me slowly slide down his body, but his arm stays around my waist, not letting me go to Riley and calm him down.

"Have you heard of knocking?" Henry's voice is all male anger and possessiveness wrapped in a neat bow.

"Why him?" Riley asks me, ignoring Henry altogether. "You were never the girl guys like him would use and move on from. You deserve more."

"Careful," Henry warns, pushing me behind him in one move as tears prick my eyes. It was almost like

Henry knew I wouldn't want Riley to see me breakdown.

Riley's overdramatic laugh fills the room. "Or fucking what?"

"Try it. I will even give you one free shot, but then your free game," Henry taunts, and I stare, frozen in horror, as Riley does just that. He takes one large step forward and smacks his fist into Henry's face, and Henry just laughs before he punches him back. Riley flies across the room from the hit, smacking against the wall.

"Stop!" I scream, running into the middle of them as Riley struggles to get up. I offer a hand to help him, but he glares at me as he gets himself up. His eyes flicker to Henry, and a sneer I've never seen on Riley crosses his face.

"I will kill you for this. One day, when you're not looking. I will fucking kill you." Riley storms out of the room, and I shout after him, only he decides to ignore me. Vesnia pops her head around the door, a worried look on her face.

"Seems like it's the night for fights," she says. "Want to walk back home with me?"

I look back at Henry as he sits on the bed, wiping the blood pouring from his nose, and he looks so pale again. Not meeting my eye, he whispers, "You should leave. I need to be alone."

"Oh, okay," I whisper back, feeling more tears waiting to fall. I take my bestie's hand and close the door behind me as I step out into the corridor. She doesn't need me to talk as she wraps me into a hug and tells me everything's going to be okay.

But it's not okay.

And if Riley doesn't let this go, it can't ever be.

CHAPTER 23

"Is he still ignoring you?" Vesnia asks as we eat breakfast. I chew my toast before leaving the rest of the meal, not feeling hungry anymore. Any mention of the two guys ignoring me makes me feel bad for not telling Thallon about my kiss with Henry. Thallon is a good guy and always honest with me, but I guess we never actually agreed we are dating. Or exclusive for that matter.

Exclusivity would mean telling Thallon the truth about the vampire ghost who haunts my room or my weird crush on the dark angel who is usually mean to me.

"Which one? Riley and Henry haven't spoken to me in over two months," I mutter in annoyance. The same can be said for Ren. I would worry he isn't around if I didn't see him every so often as I wake up or in the corridors or in the gardens. The problem is, every time he sees me, he disappears, and it's frustrating. I've always made it so, in my life, I would never once get attached to any ghost, and then Ren floats into my life, and I find myself wanting to be close to him and figure him out. I guess if I'm being honest with myself, there is a connection between us that goes unsaid, and I've never had that with a ghost before. But in the end, any feelings I may have for him are pointless because he is dead, and one day he will leave, like all the ghosts do, to go to a better or worse place.

The thought of Ren being in hell gives me a lump in my throat I have to swallow. I couldn't let him go there; he isn't evil for starters. No matter what Master Gabriel said about vampires, I know he isn't evil.

"Boys suck," she says and bumps my shoulder. "You should stick to girls."

"Of course that would be your advice," I say around a laugh.

"Being serious though, have you decided which angel you want to be?" she asks as I get up and place my tray on the bed next to her.

"I want to be a dark angel," I say, and it's not a decision I've come to lightly, but it is one I know is best for me. I've always had secrets to hide, and the price of not being able to lie would be a terrible thing for someone like me. The dark has always called to me from the first moment I came here, and the light never did. "I knew from day one, if I'm being honest. What about you?"

"I like them both, so I'm going to make the choice when I stand in front of the fires. I will see who calls to me," she tells me, and I think that's a really good decision for her. I think about me and Vesnia having wings soon and actually becoming angels. I'm so excited for us to learn how to fly on our own. As much as I love flying with Ayda, it still would be so cool to do it for myself.

"I'm excited for us both," I say, and I really mean it. "Now we best get moving to spear class. She asked us to come fifteen minutes earlier last week, remember?"

"Oh shit, yeah, I forgot," she says and shoves the last bit of toast into her mouth as I slide my trainers on. I soon figured out trainers go better with the sports gear they make us wear now. Vesnia and I head quickly to the gym on the other side of the castle, but we come to a stop when we see everyone is gathered outside.

"Brilliant, now everyone is here, follow me,"

Professor Bates says with calculating eyes. She walks us around the gym and to the end of the island where there are some stone steps going down. Nervously I look at Vesnia who shrugs, and then I search the crowd for Riley. He is right in front, and I can just about see his back. I'm hoping to talk to him today because I've heard he is sleeping with some of the light angels, and that might mean his silly crush on me is over. Maybe we can go back to being friends again?

I eye Professor Bates with some mixture of worry and fear as she is crazy, and in every lesson with her, someone has ended up getting hurt. As much as I can figure out, she has no sense of personal space and loves to see people in pain. She walks down the steps and makes it quite clear we all need to follow after her. The steps are a little wet from the rain last night as we head down one by one, and Vesnia holds onto my shoulder. We finally get to the bottom and find a long cave. Professor Bates stops at the other end, standing still even as the harsh wind blows her cloak around her. I shiver as we get into a line in front of her like we do in class.

"Angels do not fall. It is in our blood, in our bodies, in our souls and the very essence of this class and what we can teach you," she starts off and slowly turns to the side. We all stare out at the hundreds of little rocks, no bigger than four feet apart, floating around in the air. Sometimes they crash into each other, but mainly it looks like they are making small circular patterns in the wind. I get a bad feeling in the pit of my stomach before she even talks. "Today's class will be learning the art of spear fighting on these rocks. Two of you will go out one at a time, and the goal is to get to the island in the middle. If you manage to knock your opponent off, you will pass this class for the rest of the year. If you fall off, you will die as no one will catch you. Do you understand?"

"Wait, what happens if we both don't fight and just get to the middle?" I ask.

"There is only one course of rocks that get you to the middle, and they will not hold the weight of you both. You fight for the rocks, or you both die in the fall. If you both happen to work together and get to the middle, the first one to knock the other unconscious or dead wins," she answers me, and I gulp. "As you spoke first, I believe you should fight first, Miss Lightson. Mr. Becker, you will be her opponent."

"You can do this," Vesnia firmly tells me, and I nod at her as I walk forward and wish it wasn't Riley I had to go against. Especially when he is mad. I guess I'm not too worried, as I don't think Riley would actually hurt me or try to kill me, no matter how mad he is. Professor Bates gets two spears, the ones we use in class, and hands them to me as we stop near the edge. The first rock is a step away, but the others are large steps. Riley has long legs, he is going to find this a lot easier than I am.

"Good luck," I whisper to Riley and look up at him. He stares at the rocks like I'm not here and ignores me.

"Go!" Professor Bates shouts, and Riley moves first, stepping onto the rocks. He moves quick, and I step onto the rock after him. The rock wobbles under my feet, and the cold air threatens to push me off, but I make the big step onto the rock next to Riley's. I see the one rock to the left and step onto it, my throat feeling clogged with fear as it shakes a little in the wind. Taking a deep breath, I decide to step onto the smaller rock right in front of me, and it's pretty steady for a second before it tilts. I almost scream as I jump off it and onto the rock in front of me, landing face down. I crawl to my feet and look back to see Riley jumping from rock to rock to get to me. I look back, seeing four rocks in a diagonal line right up to the middle, and I know that's the best way to go. But Professor Bates is right, they are too small for anyone to do anything but step on one at a time and jump. I lean back, bracing myself just as something hard slams into my face. I scream as I fly into the air, rolling but luckily sliding across a rock. I dig my fingers and feet into the rock to stop myself and look up, knowing Riley just hit me in the face with his spear. Blood pours out of my nose as Riley looks back at me and just smiles. He turns around and takes the four steps to the middle and places his hands in the air like a champion, just before I pass out.

CHAPTER 24

I wake up alone in a white sheet-covered bed, smelling nothing but cleaning products and feeling the pain of my nose, knowing I'm going to look like crap before seeing myself in the mirror opposite me on the wall. My nose is covered in purple bruises, and it was no doubt broken. Dammit, Riley. *When did becoming an angel mean you get to be an asshat?* I sit up, blinking from the bright light just as a healer in green robes like they all wear, comes into the room.

"You are free to go. The swelling and bruising will go down in a short time," she tells me as she picks up a notebook from the end of my bed. I notice the notebook has my name on the outside of it.

"Is my friend Vesnia okay?" I question, needing

to know if she got through the class okay. I couldn't imagine a world without her in it at this point.

"The red-haired girl?" she asks as she scribbles on a notebook in her hand. "Vesnia was here, but she was ordered to return to class. You have the rest of the day off."

"Thank you," I say as she leaves the room. I make the bed before leaving the room and passing the empty rooms next door to mine before stopping when I hear a familiar voice.

"What's wrong then?" Henry demands before coughing a few times. "The nose bleeds and vision loss were getting better until recently. Something has changed."

"It seems you have become somewhat immune to this cure. We will have to search for another strand of the cure," a nervous sounding healer man replies. *So he is sick after all?*

A few more coughs fill the room. "And until then?"

"Bed rest and no stress. We will find a way to stop this—"

"Before I die and my parents hunt you down, you mean?" he snaps, and I step into the empty room as I hear their footsteps. I knew Henry was ill, and the thought hurts my heart, because there is no way he can die. I wonder for a brief moment why a healer, an angel, would be scared of human parents?

"Why are you hiding in a room?" Master Gabriel's voice makes me jump, and I knock a small plastic table over behind me.

"I wasn't," I mutter as I pick the table up and the papers that were on top of it. I put it all back together before smiling at Master Gabriel, which hurts my sore face. Master Gabriel searches my face, and a look of pity reaches his eyes for a second before he hides it.

"I was looking for you, Miss Lightson. I wondered if I could test your blood for something," he asks, folding his hands behind his back.

Odd. Why would he want my blood anyway? Surely it's like everyone else's. "For what?"

"Say no!" Ren bursts into the room, floating in front of Master Gabriel so I can hardly see him. My heart beats fast as I run my eyes over Ren, searching for what, I don't know. A ghost injury? A visual reason why he left me? I want to say a million things to Ren, like, "Hello. Nice to see you again. Where have you been? Why did you kill that vampire?" But I can't without Master Gabriel thinking I'm utterly mad and talking to myself.

"Why? I ask instead and Ren moves to stand by

the doors like he wants to run out of them or something, but his eyes never leave me.

"I was merely curious about your bloodline and ancestors. You remind me of someone, and I wish to know if it is simply a coincidence," he answers me.

"And if I am related to this someone, will you kill me?" I ask, resting against the bed in the room.

"Of course he will kill you or have someone else do it. Light angels might not be able to lie, but they are masters at avoiding the truth. Do not ignore me, Kaitlyn," Ren snaps, and I ignore the angry ghost just like he has ignored me for weeks.

"I will not kill you," Master Gabriel answers. "I am on your side, Miss Lightson. That you can trust."

I want to tell him I trust no one, and nothing, anymore. Since I've came to The Angel Academy, I feel like I've been dipped in a bucket of lies and death, and there is no one here to save me but myself.

I'm going to swim my own ass out of this bucket.

And figure out my own life.

"You can do the blood test. I don't mind," I answer more for myself. Maybe there is something in my blood that is an answer to why I can see ghosts, to why I'm not normal. I'm already in danger every day I'm at this academy, and it's only a matter of time before they find out I see ghosts. The end of The Angel Academy means going to earth and following a human around. Which means lots of new places and lots of new ghosts. I'm bound to freak out, and then everyone finds out anyway.

"Brilliant, I will go and get what I need and return," Master Gabriel states and leaves the room, brushing by Ren who glares at him.

"Nothing good will come from this," Ren warns, floating right up to me.

"Where the hell have you been?" I whisper shout, and more than ever, I wish I could hit him. "You don't get to disappear and then come back making demands about my life!"

"Did you miss me?" he asks with a cocky grin, realisation flickering in his eyes. "Oh, you did."

"You're a ghost; there is nothing to miss," I bite back.

"That says a lot about you more than it does about me," he counters. God, I hate my ghost friend right now.

Why couldn't I have an imaginary friend like all the other weirdos? At least he wouldn't abandon me and come back all cocky and shit.

"Shut up," I snap. "Why did you kill that vampire and then ignore me?"

His demeanour changes, and I can't read him for a moment. "It's safer if I stay away from you."

"What if that's not what I want?" I ask, and he shakes his head, stepping back.

"If you invite a vampire into heart, you will never get back out alive," he softly warns me before disappearing once again.

Staring at the empty room, my words are only heard by me. "Too late."

CHAPTER 25

"Did you really cook this?" I ask after swallowing another bite of the pasta and immediately getting another piece on my fork.

Thallon chuckles from the other side of the table. "I've been on my own here for years, and as much as the cooks at the academy are good, they only have a set meal. It's nice to cook something different."

"Well, I'm thankful," I reply and finish off my food. Like the perfect gentleman Thallon is, he takes my empty plate to the sink and waves off my offer to help him wash up. After cleaning up the table, I move to his sofa and sit down, curling my legs underneath me. I watch Thallon in the kitchen, noticing how his crisp white shirt reveals a lot of his muscle underneath, and how his jeans suit him. His sleeves are rolled up as he washes the dishes, which is crazy sexy to watch, and his brown hair is curlier today, like he spent time in the pouring rain that's now hitting the windows outside. Thallon Cross has the face and body of a heartbreaking boy, and for some crazy reason, I'm in his home, on a movie night date nonetheless.

"I have a gift for you. Well, two actually," he tells me before disappearing into his bedroom and coming out a few moments later.

"I don't have a gift for you," I reply as he sits down and offers me two packets of Parma Violet sweets and a DVD of *Jumanji*, my favourite movie growing up. I only told Thallon about it in a passing conversation, and I can't believe he not only remembered but got the DVD for me. I place the sweets and DVD in the middle of us before throwing my arms around his shoulders. "Thank you," I whisper into his ear, and after a while, I pull back, meeting his gaze.

"I know it's difficult to come here and leave everything behind. I wanted to make it easier for you with some home comforts," he softly tells me. "And I've never eaten a Parma Violet or watched *Jumanji*."

"We have to correct that right away," I say with

an excited chuckle. Thallon takes the DVD and goes to set it up in the DVD player as I open my sweets. I all but inhale a couple of the sweets before Thallon comes back. I take one out of the packet and hold it in the middle of my hand for him. He grins as he leans down and presses his lips around the sweet in my hand. The gentle touch of his lips makes me shiver and feel things I haven't before for any guy. I mean it wasn't like there weren't guys at my school growing up, but they never wanted anything to do with me, and I assumed I wasn't pretty for a long time. I stuck my head in books, and Riley dated half the school.

"They taste delicious," he whispers to me, and I suspect he wasn't just talking about the sweet. What the hell do I say back to that?

"I kissed Henry, and I'm feeling bad because of this"—I pause, waving between us—"I think is becoming more."

"I can't say I'm not jealous, but we never agreed to be exclusive," he replies, but his eyes betray him. They get brighter when he is mad or angry or in this case, jealous.

I pause, knowing that the same anger and jealousy burn in me. "Can I be honest?"

"Yes, always with me," he quickly answers.

"The thought of any other girl touching you makes me want to hunt them down and drop them off the side of the academy." To my surprise, he laughs, and I end up chuckling with him.

"Kaitlyn, I have no interest in anyone else," he starts off and then hesitates for a second. "I don't want to scare you off, but I really like you. If you need to figure out whatever is going on with you and Henry, then okay. I'm not going to lie and say it makes me happy, as it doesn't. It makes me want to rip his angel wings off, but I get that you need to search the connection you have with him as much as you do with me."

"I've honestly never had a relationship or any sort of one before," I admit to him. "You were my first kiss, and since then, I can't stop thinking about you."

"I'm honoured," he replies, and I sense he is being sincere even as he smiles. "And for the record, we are on a date now, and this is our third date, if I'm counting right."

"Do you include the game night with Ves?"

"I'm not sure, considering a night where your best friend ate all my food, nearly cried because she lost the board game, and then fell asleep on my sofa can be counted as a date," he answers, and I laugh.

"But I'm counting any time with you as kind of dating."

"Kind of dating," I chuckle. "I like that." My laughs die off as we stare at each other, and I don't know who moves first, but we kiss as I climb onto his lap. His hands sink into my hair as he deepens the kiss, kissing me like he is desperate for more. I glide my hands down his chest to his buttons, but he covers my hand with his, breaking the kiss.

"Kind of dating means taking this slow. As much as I want you, I want us to do this right more," he warns me.

"Right?" I breathlessly question.

"You tell me when you want more," he whispers to me, kissing me softly one more time. "And until then, I will try not to kill Henry."

"Got it," I whisper back with red cheeks. He grins, tugging me to his side as he presses play on the movie. The Angel Academy always seemed deadly, cold and downright terrifying most of the time, but in Thallon's arms, it feels like home.

CHAPTER 26

Still smiling from my evening with Thallon, I slowly walk back to the academy to go to bed. Wrapping my arms around myself thanks to the cold air, I pause when I hear a noise. I turn around just as someone grabs me and shoves something over my head. I scream, lashing out with my hands, but someone grabs them tightly and shoves a hand over my mouth. Tears fall from my eyes as I'm pulled against a hard body, and then we are in the air, that weightless feeling hard to miss. I don't struggle as I feel the cold air, knowing if I managed to get free, that falling to my death is a moot point. Eventually, my feet touch the ground, and something hard smacks into my face, knocking me to the floor.

"Don't hurt her!" Riley desperately shouts, and

hands slowly pull the covering off my face. I blink at Riley as he leans over me and offers me a hand, which I don't take. Betrayal stings like a knife as I stare at my best friend, the realisation he just had his friends kidnap me coming to light.

"What is going on?" I ask as I crawl to my feet and nearly scream at the sight of Henry on his knees, blood dripping from the dozens of cuts on his chest and face. I go running to him, but Riley catches me, holding me locked to him. Oliver and his idiotic angel friends all stand around the room, and I pause when I see two waterfalls of fire. One is white, burning white fire pouring down through the rock, and the other is black fire, spitting harshly as it sinks down into the ground. I can't stop staring at the black fire until Riley grabs my chin and turns my face to his.

"We are graduating early, baby," he says, and I snap my head from his grip. I smack my hands against his chest until he lets go and nods to his friends. They rush over and grab an arm each, holding on tightly so I can't move. They laugh between themselves, and I realise somehow Riley has become their little gang leader.

How did that even happen? He isn't even an angel yet!

"Let me and Henry go. Why are you doing this? Whatever *this* is!" I shout at Riley. "I used to love you like a brother, and now you are ruining that!"

Riley looks back at me once, a cool and determined expression on his face. "Just watch."

I stay frozen as Riley walks headfirst into the white fire, and time seems to stand still. Every breath of mine is laboured as nothing happens, and then Riley appears. He walks out of the fire, letting white embers drop off his new white wings with every step he takes. Only the white fire and the light angel don't call to me, my gaze drifts to the black fire, wishing I could run headfirst into it.

Riley is laughing like a mad man until he suddenly stops, and his words are even crazier. "I am a light angel, and you are my mate, Kaitlyn Lightson."

"Mate?" I question in a daze, still staring at the black fire.

Riley with his kind eyes and evil heart walks right up to me, and the hands holding me let go. Good little slaves he has there.

"Angels have soul mates, and the only way we can be together is if you become a light angel."

"You're not my soulmate, and I never want to be a light angel. I'm sorry, but I know what my choice is,"

I tell him, feeling stronger than I am right in this moment.

"Who said you get a choice?" he asks and laughs like the cruel boy he truly is. Becoming an angel changed my best friend into a monster, and I ignored it because I couldn't face it yet.

And I'm a fool.

"Fine, I will do what you want if you let Henry go," I say, still eyeing Henry who looks worse by the minute. "He doesn't deserve to die because of me. Just let him go."

"We aren't negotiating, and I'm never going to let Henry go. He dies tonight, just after he sees you turned into a light angel."

CHAPTER 27

"No!" I scream at Riley, the utter lunatic. "Even if I was a light angel, I will never love you. I will never be your mate."

"You will love me in time, when you forget about him and that gardener," he sneers. "We can go back to our town and be together like we were. I always knew we would end up together; I made sure no guy in the school would date you. Other than Jordon, but he was a tool." He shakes his head. "That doesn't matter now, because we live in a world where we can be mated forever. We will be together forever because the light above wants that for us. Why else would we have died together at the same time? It was a sign."

"I don't love you like that, and I never will. If you kill Henry and Thallon, I still won't love you," I softly tell him. "This isn't the way to get what you want, and we both know it."

"But you do love me more than them. I'm the only one who knows all your secrets, understands your past, understands you!"

"That is because you were my best friend!" I scream back, tears falling into my lips. Their salty burn is all I can focus on for a second.

"It's because I'm meant to be your mate, and you will see that soon enough."

"Let her go!" Henry roars, and I run to him, falling on my knees as close as I can get to him.

Riley's hand falls on my shoulder, and I roughly push him off me. "You have a minute to say goodbye."

Searching Henry's angry eyes, I haven't a clue what to say. "I don't know how to get us out of this."

"Maybe this is the end for us," he almost jokes, and it makes me smile, despite everything. "I always knew you would be trouble, darlin'."

I frown because the thought of Henry and me never seeing each other again seems impossible.

"Never-ending sounds a lot better for us. We are both too stubborn to give up easily."

"Run, fight, do something. Don't let him win," Henry whispers to me, and in his eyes, I see the moment he decides to ask me one more thing, even when it means telling me another secret. "Call Erendriel and see if he can help."

"How do you know Ren?" I whisper in pure shock, and Henry's eyes give it all away. He knows my secret, he always did.

And he knows who Ren is and likely more secrets I wouldn't even know to ask for.

"Minute is up," Riley states as he grabs my arm. "In fact, our time is up."

"No, no, no!" I scream as Riley effortlessly drags me towards the fire waterfalls until I can feel their heat on my skin. I struggle, tugging at his hand on my upper arm, hitting his chest and face, but he is like a stone.

"We will see how you feel when you come out of this," Riley whispers to me.

"REN!" I scream as Riley pushes me forward, and I start to fall. I twist around just as Ren appears so close to me and reaches both his hands out to catch me, even when he can't. As I fall into the fire and it burns my back, I grab Ren's hand, and somehow we touch, and I drag him into light angel fire with me.

CHAPTER 28

Bright white light burns in front of my eyes as I sit in a pool of white fire. It flickers around me, almost like a dance, never hurting me like I suspected it would.

Almost like I wish it would.

"I didn't choose the light."

My words seem to echo around the fire, and they don't respond. The white fire seems endless, and I wonder if I'm going to die now.

I don't know if life as a light angel would be worth living at this point.

My best friend is a monster who betrayed me in the worst way.

Henry and Thallon might be seriously hurt, if not dead.

My parents don't remember who I am.

Even I don't know who I am anymore.

"You're mine." I look up to see Ren, not ghost Ren, but he is real as he walks through the flames to me. His clothes are the same, still torn in places and very outdated. His skin is no longer a ghostly pale, but flushed and tanned. Everything about Ren is more like this, and it makes me wonder if I'm really dead now. Maybe the white fire killed me, knowing this wasn't the future I wanted. Tears form in the corners of my eyes as he picks me up off the fire floor and holds me to him. Ren walks, still holding me, through the fire even as it hits his skin, and he flinches. He still keeps walking as he grits his teeth, and I hold onto his neck. Without realising it, large white wings cover Ren and me.

My wings.

I stare up at them as they shield me and Ren from the fires, the soft feather wings not being damaged at all. I have wings now, and yes, they might not be what I wanted, but I can't deny how truly lovely they are.

Soon the bright white fire is gone, and cold air blasts against my back where my T-shirt must be ripped.

"Who are you?" Riley demands as Ren gently places me on the ground outside the fire. He is real, it's not just me that sees him anymore. Ren moves quicker than I can track, punching Riley so hard that he is instantly knocked out on the floor. In less than five minutes, Ren has all Riley's friends on the floor, and I don't even care if they are breathing.

"It worked," Henry's voice says in the distance, like he doesn't believe it any more than I do.

Ren laughs. "You look like shit."

"I'm not dead yet," he laughs back, like they are long lost friends or something. What world have I just walked back into?

"How do you two know each other?" I ask, standing up despite how weak and dizzy I feel. "Wait, how are you *alive*, Ren?"

Both of them pause and look at me, and yet I can't read their expressions. Guilt? Longing? Wishing to speak more lies? "I will explain everything soon, my Kaitlyn."

I shake my head at Ren's bullshit answer as he breaks the chains off Henry's wrists like they are nothing more than paper. "Now, my subject, kill these angels and meet me above with the coven."

Henry bows his head, coughing on his blood. "Yes, my lord."

"Not Riley!" I shout, rushing over to them and stumbling on my wings. God, these things are a trip hazard. Ren catches me, pulling me to his chest and tutting under his breath. Shadows drift around our feet before engulfing us into darkness, much like what Henry did that one time. When we reappear, we are in a room I don't know with ten glowing angel-shaped orbs. Ren lets me go, and I stumble back.

"How?" I ask again as Ren walks to the first orb and snatches it. He crushes it in his hand before moving onto the next. A blasting alarm rings across the academy, and soon the sounds of screaming, breaking windows and shouts fill the once silent academy.

"Erendriel Raloxisys, don't you dare ignore me!" I scream at him, and he pauses on the fourth orb. I mentally thank old me for learning his crazy name now.

Ren's eyes are no longer the colour of a starless sky, now they have all the stars in them, and I feel like I'm in a different galaxy altogether. This has all been a game played by everyone I know, and I've been playing a different sport all this time. "All the answers will be given to you once the academy is secure."

"No! I want them now!" I scream and run to the door. I hear Ren cursing behind me just as I get to the handle and pull it open. The corridor of the academy is familiar and full of students as they run away. Master Gabriel runs past me, his eyes going above my head to no doubt see Ren.

"It's been a long time coming, Master Gabriel. I did promise revenge as I died," Ren says from right behind me, and I turn around, doing the only thing I can think of. I lean up and press my lips to Ren's.

He stays so still for a long time, like a statue.

Like my ghost. Like he isn't real, and I'm kissing nothing but air.

But then he moves and kisses me back, pulling me into his arms and into the room. My back hits the wall just as he pulls away and tuts.

"I know what you just did," Ren whispers to me, brushing his lips against mine once more. "And I'm never letting you go now."

I run a finger down his cheek, shocked still that he is real. "Why me?"

"The most powerful vampires in history all had one gift. It was given to them by the gods, and only their bloodline could use it. Can you guess what it was?" he asks me. I don't think now is time for a history lesson. Only, as he stares at me, it suddenly snaps into place.

"To see ghosts?"

"Correct, my little angel hybrid," he whispers to me. Tears fall down my cheek, and he kisses them away like they are his to claim. "A prophecy once spoke of a union between angels and vampires. I came here years ago to try and make the prophecy come true, but they murdered me, and there was nothing but darkness until you came here. Now I know the prophecy was talking about you, Kaitlyn Lightson."

"And what does it say?" I gasp.

"That once you're a vampire, albeit a half, you will be mine." He roughly turns my head to the side and presses his body into mine so hard that I can't move. "And then, my queen, we will rule every single world." He slams his sharp teeth into my neck, and I scream.

EPILOGUE

I thought dying once was the worst kind of pain I've ever been in, but as I open my eyes, looking up at the unfamiliar bedroom ceiling, I know I was wrong. From my neck to every part of my body, I can feel nothing but a life crushing pain.

The pain in my soul is the worst. It's crushing me, hurting me, and I know I need to do something.

I push the sheets on top of me back on the bed and slide my aching legs off the side. I crawl to the door but pause as I hear *his* voice outside.

"Make sure no one goes in there. I will be back soon."

Ren.

The master vampire and no longer my friendly ghost I thought I could trust. Betrayal claws deep into my heart as I turn around and look at the balcony outside this room. Walking outside, I push the glass door open and stand on the edge of the balcony, looking down at the skies below. Deep clouds, beautiful rain and endless night are all I can see. I'm in a tower, and nothing and no one is going to stop me now. I look over my shoulder at my beautiful wings.

I may be an angel.

But now...now I fall, and I won't save myself. Climbing on the bannister of the balcony, not one bit of fear trickles into my soul as I jump and let the cold air of night swallow my scream.

Pre-order the next part of the story by clicking here.

NOTE FROM THE AUTHOR.

Hello my lovely readers. There are so many people I need to thank for making my books happen, especially this world. I wrote the first book in this world, Tales & Time, over two years ago and I never planned to be still writing in this world now. The characters came rushing at me out of nowhere and demanded their story was told. I hope you have enjoyed Madi's and Anastasia's story, and the start of Kaitlyn's.

The end of this three book series will mark the end of this world, and I do hope you love what happens next!

A big thank you to my family who have always been there for me and everyone that supported me with this book. Even if it was simply liking my teasers/covers or popping me a message to say how much you loved the books so far. Every message, post, and review gives me so much happiness.

A special thank you my editor, Helayna and Mads, my personal assistant! They are my life savers and I couldn't do this without them.

Special thank you to Bailey's Pack and all it's wonderful members. Your love for my books gives me life.

If you have the time, a small review would be very much appreciated. I read every one, and always have done.

Happy Future Reading!! Love G. xoxo

The Missing Wolf. Please carry on reading for small excerpt.

Leaving the past behind.

Anastasia

I stand still on the side of the train tracks, letting the cold wind blow my blonde and purple dip-dyed hair across my face. I squeeze the handle of my suitcase tighter, hoping that the train will come soon. *It's freezing today, and my coat is packed away in the suitcase, dammit.* I feel like I've waited for this day for years, the day I get to leave my foster home and join my sister at college. I look behind me into the parking lot, seeing my younger sister stood watching me go, my foster grandmother holding her hand. Phoebe is only eleven years old, but she is acting strong today, no matter how much she wants me to stay. I smile at her, trying to ignore how difficult it feels to leave her here, but I know she couldn't be in a better home. I can get through college with our older sister and then get a job in the city, while living all together. *That's the plan anyway.*

We lost our mum and dad in a car accident ten years ago, and we were more than lucky to find a foster parent that would take all three of us in. Grandma Pops is a special kind of lady. She is kind and loves to cook, and the money she gets from fostering pays for her house. She lost her two children in a fire years ago, and she tells us regularly that we keep her happy and alive. Even if we do eat a lot for three kids. Luckily, she likes to look after us as I burn everything I attempt to cook. And I don't even want to remember the time I tried to wash my clothes, which ended in disaster.

"Train four-one-nine to Liverpool is calling at the station in one minute," the man announces over the loudspeaker, just before I hear the sound of the train coming in from a distance. I turn back to see the grey train speeding towards us, only slowing down when it gets close, but I still have to walk to get to the end carriage. I wait for the two men in front of me to get on before I step onto the carriage, turning to pull my suitcase on. I search through the full seats until I find an empty one near the back, next to a window. I have to make sure it's facing the way the train is going as it freaks me out to sit the other way. I slide my suitcase under the seat before sitting down, leaving my handbag on the small table in front of me.

I wave goodbye to my sister, who waves back, her head hidden on grandma's shoulder as she cries. I can only see her waist length, wavy blonde hair before the train pulls away. I'm going to miss her. *Urgh, it's not like we don't have phones and FaceTime!* I'm being silly. I pull my phone out of my bag and quickly send a message to my older sis, letting her know I am on the train. I also send a message to Phoebe, telling her how much I love and miss her already.

"Ticket?" the train employee guy asks, making me jump out of my skin, and my phone falls on the floor.

"Sorry! I'm always dropping stuff," I say, and the man just stares at me with a serious expression, still holding his hand out. His uniform is crisply ironed, and his hair is combed to the left without a single hair out of place. I roll my eyes and pull my bag open, pulling out my ticket and handing it to him. After he checks it for about a minute, he scribbles on it before handing it back to me. I've never understood why they bother drawing on the tickets when the machines check the tickets at the other end anyway. I put my ticket back into my bag before sliding it under the seat just as the train moves, jolting me a little.

I reach for my phone, which is stuck to some paper underneath it. I've always been taught to pick up rubbish, so I grab the paper as well as my phone before slipping out from under the table and back to my seat. I put my phone back into my handbag before looking at the leaflet I've picked up. It's one of those warning leaflets about familiars and how it is illegal to hide one. The leaflet has a giant lion symbol at the top and warning signs around the edges. It explains that you have to call the police and report them if you find one.

Familiars account for 0.003 percent of the human race, though many say they are nothing like humans and don't like to count them as such. Familiars randomly started appearing about fifty years ago, or at least publicly they did. A lot of people believe they just kept themselves hidden before that.

The Familiar Empire was soon set up, and it is the only place safe for familiars to live in peace. They have their own laws, an alliance with humans, and their own land in Scotland, Spain and North America.

Unfortunately, anyone could suddenly become a familiar, and you wouldn't know until one random day. It can be anything from a car crash to simply waking up that sets off the gene, but once a familiar, always a familiar. They have the mark on their hand, a glowing tattoo of whatever animal is bonded to them. The animals are the main reason familiars are so dangerous. They have a bond with one animal who would do anything for them. Even kill. And I heard once that some kid's animal was a lion as big as an elephant. But those are just the things we know publicly, who knows what is hidden behind the giant walls of the Familiar Empire?

"My uncle is one, you know?" a girl says, and I look up to see a young girl about ten years old hanging over her seat, her head tilted to the side as she stares at the leaflet in my hand. "He has a big rabbit for a familiar."

"That's awesome..." I say, smiling as I put the leaflet down. I bet picking up giant rabbit poo isn't that awesome, but I don't tell her that.

"I want to be a familiar when I grow up," she excitedly says. "They have cool powers and pets! Mum won't even let me get a dog!"

"Sit down, Clara! Stop talking to strangers!" her mum says, tugging the girl's arm, and she sits down after flashing me a cheeky grin.

I fold the leaflet and slide it into my bag before resting back in the seat, watching the city flash by from the window. I couldn't think of anything worse than being a familiar. You have to leave your family, your whole life, and live in the woods. *Being a familiar seems like nothing but a curse.*

FIND THE MISSING WOLF HERE...

Who wears a cloak these days?

"Ana!!" my sister practically screeches as I step off the train, and then throws herself at me before I get a second to really look at her. Even though my sister is only a few inches taller than my five-foot-four self, she nearly knocks me over. I pull her blonde hair away from my face as it tries to suffocate me before she thankfully pulls away. I'm not a hugger, but Bethany always ignores that little fact.

"I missed you too, Bethany," I mutter, and she grins at me. Bethany was always the beautiful sister, and as we got older, she just got prettier. Seems the year at college has only added to that. Her blonde hair is almost white, falling in perfect waves down her back. Mine is the same, but I dyed the ends a deep purple. Another one of my attempts at sticking out in a crowd when I usually become invisible next to my gorgeous sister. Phoebe is the image of Bethany, and both of them look like photos of our mother. Whereas I look like my dad mostly, I still have the blonde hair. Bethany grins at me, then slowly runs her eyes over my outfit before letting out a long sigh.

"You look so pretty, sis," she says, and I roll my eyes. Bethany hates jeans and long-sleeved tops, which I happen to be wearing both. I didn't even look at what I threw on this morning. I shiver as the cold wind blows around me, reminding me that I should have gotten my coat out my suitcase on the train trip. It is autumn.

"You're such a bad liar," I reply, arching an eyebrow at her, and she laughs.

"Well, you are eighteen now, and I've never seen you in a dress. College is going to change all that." She waves a hand like she has sorted all the problems out.

"How so? I'm not wearing a dress to classes," I say, frowning at her. "Leggings are much easier to run around in, I think."

"Parties, of course," she tuts, laughing like it should be obvious. Bethany grabs hold of my suitcase before walking down the now empty sidewalk to the parking lot at the end.

"I need to study. There is no way I'm going to ace my nursing classes without a lot of studying," I tell her. Bethany took drama, and I wasn't the least bit surprised when she was offered a job at the end of her course, depending on her grades. Though she was an A-star student throughout high school, so there is no way she could fail.

"I love that you will have the same job mum did," she eventually tells me, and I glance over at her as she smiles sadly at me before focusing back on where she is walking. I remember my mum and dad, whereas Bethany is just over one year older than me and remembers a lot more. Phoebe doesn't remember them at all; she only has our photos and the things we can tell her. It was difficult for Bethany to leave us both to come to college, but grandma and I told her she had to find a future.

"I doubt I will do it as well as her...but I like to

help people. I know this is the right thing for me to do," I reply, and I see her nod in the corner of my eye. I quickly walk forward and hold the metal gate to the car park open for Bethany to walk through before catching up with her as we walk past cars.

"You've always been the nice one. I remember when you were twelve, and the boy down the road broke up with you because some other girl asked him out. The next day, that boy fell off his bike, cutting all his leg just outside our home. You helped him into the house, put plasters on his leg, and then walked his bike back to his house for him," she remarks. "Most people wouldn't have done that. I would have just laughed at him before leaving him on the sidewalk."

"I also called him a dumbass," I say, laughing at the memory of his shocked face. "So I wasn't all that nice."

"That's why you are so amazing, sis," she laughs, and I chuckle as we get to Bethany's car. It's a run down, black Ford Fiesta, but I know Bethany adores the old thing. Even if there are scratches and bumps all over the poor car from Bethany's terrible driving.

"Get in, I can put the suitcase in the boot," she says, and I pull the passenger door open before sliding inside. I do my seatbelt up before resting back, watching out of the passenger window at the train pulling out of the station. There is a man in a black cloak stood still in the middle of the path, the wind pushing his cloak around his legs, but his hood is up, covering his face. I just stare, feeling stranger and more freaked out by the second as the man lifts his head. I see a flash of yellow under his hood for a brief moment, and I sit forward, trying to see more of the strange man I can't pull my eyes from. I almost jump out of my skin when Bethany gets in the car, slamming her door shut behind her, and I look over at her.

"Are you okay? You look pale," she asks, reaching over to put her hand on my head to check my temperature before pulling it away. I look back towards the man, seeing that he and the train are gone. Everything is quiet, still and creepy. *Time to go.*

"Yeah, everything is fine. I'm just nervous about my first day," I tell her, which is sort of honest, but I'm missing the little fact about the weird hooded man. *I mean, who walks around in cloaks like friggin' Darth Vader?* She frowns at me, seeing through my lies easily, but after I don't say a word for a while, she drops it.

"It will be fine. Don't worry!" she says, reaching

over to squeeze my hand before starting the car. I keep my eyes on the spot the man was in until I can't see it anymore. I close my eyes and shake my head, knowing it was just a creepy guy, and I need to forget it. This is my first day of my new life, and nothing is going to ruin that.

One moment can change everything.

"Anastasia Noble?" I hear someone shout out as I wait in the middle of the crowd of new students. Bethany left me here about half an hour ago, and she is going to find me later once I have my room sorted. First, I have to get through a tour of the university, even though I had a tour here when I visited two months ago. I also spent days studying the map they gave me, so I know where I am going. Putting my hand in the air, I move through the crowd, pulling my suitcase behind me with my arm starting to ache from lugging the giant purple suitcase everywhere.

I get to the front of the crowd, where an older man waves me over. I quickly make my way to him and the three other students waiting at his side. Two of them are girls, both blonde and whispering between themselves with their pink suitcases. The other is a guy who is too interested in ogling the blondes to notice me coming over. Story of my life right there. I stop right in front of the older man who stinks of too much cologne, and I shake his slightly sweaty hand before stepping back.

"Welcome to Liverpool University. We are the smallest, but fiercest, university in northern England. Now, I am going to show you around the basic area before taking you to your rooms. You all will share a corridor and living area, so look around at your new friends and maybe say hello!" the man says, clapping his hands together before quickly turning to walk away. We all jog to catch up with him as he walks us across the grass towards one of the buildings on either side of the clearing.

There is a little river in the middle with planted flowers and trees all surrounding it. It's peaceful, exactly why my sister chose this university, I suspect. She always likes seeing the beauty in life, where I am always looking for a way to fix the world instead. I wish we had other family around that could tell us about what our parents were like, who each of us follow, or if we are just random in the family line of personalities. We don't even know if our parents had any close friends. There is nothing much in our foster pack given to grandma from social services. Bethany and I talked about going to the village we lived in to ask around, but neither of us ever found the time.

"Anastasia, right?" a guy asks, slowing down to walk at my side. He has messy brown hair, blue eyes, and a big rucksack on his back.

"Yep, who are you?" I ask.

"Don. Nice to meet you," he replies, offering me a hand to shake with a big grin. I shake his hand before looking up at the massive archway we are walking through to get inside of the building. It is two smooth pillars meeting together in the middle. There are old gargoyle statues lining the archway, their creepy eyes staring down at me. Those statues always creep me out. Bethany thinks it's funny, so last Christmas, she got me gargoyle romance books as a joke. Jokes on her though; some of those books were damn good. I quickly look away, back to where we are walking, as Don starts talking again.

"I've heard there is a party tonight to welcome freshers. Are you going?" he asks me, his arm annoyingly brushing against mine with how closely he has decided to walk. I glance up at him to see his gaze is firmly focused on my breasts rather than my face.

"No. I need to unpack," I curtly reply.

"Can't it wait one night?" he asks, and I look over at him once again. He is gorgeous, but the whiney attitude about a party is a big turn off. "I will make sure you have fun."

"No. It can't wait, and I doubt anything you could do would make the party fun for me," I say honestly, and not shockingly, he nods before catching up with the two blonde girls in the group, trying his pickup techniques on them. *Men.*

Bethany says I'm picky, but actually, it's just because the general male population at my age are idiots and act like kids most of the time too. I don't see how anyone could want to date them, though Bethany is on her twelfth boyfriend since she came to college, so I know she doesn't share my opinion. She swears she will know when the right guy comes along, and it will be the same for me. I doubt it. Anyway, finding the "right" guy is not the most important thing at the moment; passing college and getting my nursing degree is.

"This is the oldest part of the university and where most the lessons are. In the welcome packs

sent to your old homes were the links to an app
which is a map. It will help you find your lessons,"
the tour guide explains before opening a door out of
the old corridor and into another one which is more
modern. There are white-tiled floors, lockers lining
the walls, and spotlights in the ceiling that shine so
brightly everything gleams. "Every student gets a
locker here, which is perfect for storing books and
anything you don't need for every class. Trust me,
you will get a lot of books, so the lockers are a
godsend."

We walk down the corridor, listening to the
guide explain the history of the university when
suddenly there is a burning feeling in my hand that
comes out of nowhere. I scream, dropping to my
knees as I grab my hand, trying to stop the incredible pain. I rub at my pale skin as it burns hot, yet
there is nothing there to see. The pain gets worse
until I can't see or hear anything for a moment, and I
fall back. When I blink my eyes open, I'm lying on
the cold floor, hearing the chatter of students near
me. No one is helping me, oddly enough, and they
sound like they are far away. Every part of my body
hurts, aches like I've been running a marathon.

"She's a familiar. Has anyone called the police?"

one person asks as I stare up at the flickering spotlight right above me.

"We should leave; she could hurt us. Who knows where her creature is!" another man harshly whispers. I lift my hand above my face almost in slow motion. My eyes widen in pure shock at the huge, glowing, purple wolf tattoo covering the back of my hand where it burned. It stops at my wrist, the wolf's fur extending halfway up my fingers and thumb. The eyes of the wolf tattoo glow the brightest as I realise what this means.

"I'm a familiar."

Time to run before it is too late.

s soon as I've said it out loud, it feels like I can't breathe as I sit up and look around at the people staring at me. The group I was with are huddled by the lockers a good distance away from me now, and I turn to see more people have shown up, a few of them on their phones. All of them are scared, worried what I will do as they keep their eyes on me. They are going to call the police and have me taken away because of this. *I have to get to Bethany first.* I have to at least say goodbye to her before they come for me and take me some place where I may never see her again.

I quickly scramble to my feet and run down the corridor, passing everyone who shouts for me to stop, until I get to the door at the end. I push it open, running through the arch and into the empty clearing. Stopping by the river, I look up and quickly try to remember how to get to the dorms. Shit, I don't even know what room she is in. I pull my handbag off my shoulder to get my phone out just as I hear a low growl from right behind me.

I slowly drop my bag onto the floor and turn around, seeing a giant wolf inches away from my face. The wolf is taller than I am; its head is leant down so I can see into its stunning blue eyes. They remind me of my own eyes, to be honest, with little swirls of black, light and dark blues, all mixed together. My body and mind seem to relax as I stare at the creature, one which I should be terrified of... but I am not. I feel myself moving my hand up, and then the wolf growls a little, shaking me out of that thought.

I step back, which only seems to piss her or him off more. Some deep part of me knows I have to touch the wolf now, or I will always regret it. I take a deep breath before stepping closer and quickly placing my hand on the middle of the wolf's forehead. I didn't notice it was my hand with the familiar mark on it until this point, until it glows so brightly purple that I have to turn my head away. When the light dims, I look back to see the black wolf staring at me as I lower my hand.

"Your name is Shadow," I say out loud, though I don't have a clue how I know that, but I know it is true. Shadow bows his head before lying on the ground in front of me. He is my familiar. *That's how I know.* That's why I am not scared of the enormous wolf like I should be. I have a gigantic wolf for my familiar. *Holy crap.* It takes me a few seconds to pull my gaze from Shadow and remember what I was going to do. Find my sister, that's what.

"We need to find my sister...can you help me? Like smell her, maybe? She smells like me," I ask Shadow and then realise I have no clue if he can understand me. Shadow looks up, tilting his head to the side before stretching out, knocking his head into my stomach. I step back, sighing. "Never mind."

Shadow growls at me, and I give him a questioning look. What is up with the growling? I thought familiar animals were meant to be familiars' best friends or something. I really get the feeling Shadow isn't all that impressed with me. He shakes his giant head before walking around me and slowly running off in the direction of the other building.

"Wait up!" I have to run fast to catch up with him as he gets to the front of the university, people moving fast out of his way and some even screaming. I don't even blame them. A giant black wolf running towards you is not something you see every day. I run faster, getting to Shadow's side as we round a corner, and I hear Bethany's laugh just before I see her sat on a bench with a guy. They both turn with wide, scared eyes to us, and the guy falls back off the bench before running away.

The sounds of people's screaming, shouting and general fear drift into nothing but silence as I meet my sister's eyes as she stands up. A tear streams down her cheek, saying everything neither one of us can speak. I will be made to leave her, and I have no idea when—if ever—I will get to see her again. Bethany is the first to move, running to me and wrapping her arms around my shoulders. She doesn't even look at Shadow; she doesn't fear me either, which is a huge relief. I hug her back, trying to commit every part of her to my memory as I try not to cry. *I have to be strong.* If I break down now, Bethany will never be able to cope. I pull back as I hear sirens in the background and know my time here is coming to an end.

"I will find a way back to you. I will never stop

until I do. Just look after yourself and Phoebe. Promise me?" I ask Bethany, holding my hands on her shoulders as she sobs.

"I promise. If anyone can work out a way around the rules, it's you. I love you, sis," she says, crying her eyes out between each word. I hug her once more before stepping back to Shadow's side, away from my sister and my old life. "Be safe."

"Go. Just go, I don't want you to see me arrested or how nasty the police are to familiars. The YouTube videos are enough," I say, but Bethany shakes her head, wiping her cheeks and crossing her arms. I've accidently seen enough videos online to know that the police, the government and the general population are not nice to new familiars. That's why they are taken straight away. I'm not going to fight or try to run like some familiars do. I doubt I would get far with Shadow at my side.

"I am staying until they take you. You will not be alone," she says as I hear shouting and the sounds of dozens of feet running towards us. I gasp as I feel a sharp prick in the side of my neck, and Bethany screams. Shadow growls, which turns into a howl as I try to reach for him as he falls to the ground at my side. The world turns to blackness, and the last thing

I hear is Bethany's pleas for someone to leave me alone.

STAY IN TOUCH AND GET SOME FREE BOOKS!

SIGN UP TO MY NEWSLETTER FOR FREE BOOKS,

TEASERS, GIVEAWAYS AND MORE...

SIGN UP HERE.

FOLLOW ME ON INSTAGRAM-

Instagram

FIND ME ON FACEBOOK-

Facebook

TWITTER IS ALWAYS FUN-

Twitter

WANT TO SEE THE BOARDS FULL OF MY IDEAS-

Pinterest

FIND ALL MY BOOKS HERE-

www.gbaileyauthor.com

ABOUT THE AUTHOR

G. Bailey is a USA Today and international bestselling author of books that are filled with everything from dragons to pirates. Plus, fantasy worlds and breath-taking adventures.

G. Bailey is from the very rainy U.K. where she lives with her husband, two children, three cheeky dogs and one cat who rules them all.

A few random facts about her...

She loves tea. (She may be a little obsessed but what Brit isn't?)

Chocolate and Harry Potter marathons are her jam.

She owns way too many notebooks and random pens.

Please feel free say hello on here or head over to Facebook to join G. Bailey's group, Bailey's Pack! (Where you can find exclusive teasers, random giveaways and sneak peeks of new books on the way!)

FIND MORE BOOKS BY G. BAILEY ON AMAZON...
LINK HERE.